Heaven Eyes

David Almond

Hodder
Children's
Books
a division of Hodder Headline Limited

Thanks for the support of Southlands School

First published in Great Britain in 2000
by Hodder Children's Books
a division of Hodder Headline Limited
338 Euston Road
London NW1 3BH

5 7 9 10 8 6 4

A Catalogue record for this book is available
from the British Library

ISBN 0 340 74368 9

Typeset by Avon Dataset Ltd, Bidford-on-Avon, Warks

Printed and bound in Great Britain by
Clays Ltd, St Ives plc

About the Author

David Almond's debut novel *Skellig* is one of the most remarkable children's novels published in recent years. It won the 1998 Whitbread Children's Book of the Year and the Carnegie Medal. *Kit's Wilderness*, his second novel, was published to similar acclaim. *Heaven Eyes* is his third novel for children.

'I grew up in a big family in a small steep town overlooking the River Tyne. It was a place of ancient coal mines, dark terraced streets, strange shops, new estates and wild heather hills. Our lives were filled with mysterious and unexpected events, and the place and its people have given me many of my stories. I always wanted to be a writer, though I told very few people until I was "grown up". I write for adults as well as children. I've been a postman, a brush salesman, an editor and a teacher. I've lived by the North Sea, in inner Manchester, in a Suffolk farmhouse, and I wrote my first stories in a remote and dilapidated Norfolk mansion.

Writing can be difficult, but sometimes it really does feel like a kind of magic. I think that stories are living things – among the most important things in the world.'

David Almond

Also by David Almond

Skellig
Kit's Wilderness

Other books published by Hodder Signature:

The Fated Sky
Chance of Safety
Henrietta Branford

Strays Like Us
Richard Peck

Moving Times
Rachel Anderson

Telling Tales
Susan Price

Secret Songs
Jane Stemp

For Jim and Kathleen Almond

PART ONE

WHITEGATES

One

My name is Erin Law. My friends are January Carr and Mouse Gullane. This is the story of what happened when we sailed away from Whitegates that Friday night. Some people will tell you that none of these things happened. They'll say they were just a dream that the three of us shared. But they did happen. We did meet Heaven Eyes on the Black Middens. We did dig the saint out of the mud. We did find Grampa's treasures and his secrets. We did see Grampa return to the river. And we did bring Heaven Eyes home with us. She lives happily here among us. People will tell you that this is not Heaven Eyes. They'll say she's just another damaged child like ourselves. But she is Heaven Eyes. You'll know her easily. Look at her toes and fingers. Listen to her strange sweet voice. Watch how she seems to see through all the darkness in the world to the joy that lies beneath. It is her. These things happened. January, Mouse and I were there to see them all. Everything is true. So listen.

We are damaged children. Each of us has lost our parents. That's why we live in this home called Whitegates, which is in St Gabriel's Estate. January, for instance, was left as a day-old baby on the steps of a hospital. He's called January because that's the bitter month in which he was found. The place was Carr Hill Hospital, and that's why he's called Carr. You will not see January here now, and you'll know why when you come to the end of the tale. Mouse is an abandoned boy. His mother died, like mine did, and then his father disappeared. Mouse will tell you that his father's in Africa, but even Mouse isn't certain that this is true. He's named Mouse because of the pet he carries in his pocket, which he used to say was his one true friend. This pet is called Squeak, because he squeaks.

Whitegates is a three-storeyed place with a garden laid to concrete and a metal fence around it. The home is run by a woman named Maureen. Before we sailed away that night, her heart had been disappointed by years of dealing with children like ourselves. She used to tell us we were damaged. She said that, right from the start, our opportunities were more limited than those of other children. She said we'd have to work very hard to make our way in the world. She smiled and stroked our shoulders. She said that if we co-operated with her, there was no reason why we shouldn't turn out to be the finest of folk. Sometimes we saw in her eyes that she really wanted to believe this. Sometimes we saw that she yearned to believe. She gazed from the windows and watched us whispering together in the concrete garden. She stood in the doorway of the pool room and watched us with her fingers on her cheeks and the yearning in her eyes.

She has a flat behind her office and she was often heard whimpering in there. She found it difficult to sleep in those days. Sometimes we saw her wandering the corridors in the dead of night with tears running from her eyes. There were many tales and rumours about her: she'd never been able to have children of her own; yes, she did have a child, and it was very beautiful, but it died as a baby in her arms; there were several children, but they'd been snatched away by the father and had never been seen again. No one knew the truth, but we made up the tales and told them to each other and tried to explain the strange mixture of love and bitterness we saw in Maureen's eyes. Those eyes so often were cold, cold, cold. Those eyes wanted to love us and trust us, but so often they saw us as simply damaged, and beyond repair.

A dozen or so children live here. Some of us, like Maureen, are filled by sadness, or eaten up with bitterness. Some of us have broken hearts and troubled souls. But most of us love each other and look out for each other. We always knew that if we cared for each other, we could put up with the psychiatrists who came, the psychologists, the social workers, the care workers, the play workers, the drugs workers, the health workers, the welfare workers. We knew we could put up with Maureen with her assistants. We could put up with her questions and her coldness and her circle times. We knew that we could find a tiny corner of the Paradise that we'd all lost.

Sometimes we were asked to go back to that Paradise. We were asked to try to imagine how things were for us before we were in Whitegates. We had circle times. We sat together in the lounge. Maureen told us what was known about each of us: who our mothers were, who our fathers were, what happened to separate us from them. For some of us, of course, very little was known. She asked us to tell what we remembered. Her assistants, Fat Kev and Skinny Stu, paced the floor behind us and encouraged us to speak. Maureen asked us to imagine the things that weren't remembered or known. She said it was important that each of us could tell the story of our life, even if it was a mixture of fact and memory and imagination. Each of us had a Life Story book with photographs, drawings, facts and stories in them. Some children played this game very well. They could imagine a different story every time. Their books were filled with possible stories and possible lives. Some children were sullen and would not play, and their books were almost empty.

January quickly became one of those who wouldn't play. But once he told the story of a frantic woman in a stormy winter night. She was very young and very beautiful and very desperate. She carried a tiny baby wrapped in blankets in an orange box. She loved the baby very much but knew she couldn't care for him. She kept in the shadows as she approached the hospital. She waited for deepest night, trembling with cold, with pain, with love. Then she hurried through the storm and laid him on the wide doorstep before rushing back into the night.

'That was beautiful,' Maureen said.

She reached out and stroked his brow.

'It could well be true,' she whispered.

January stared at her. His eyes were glittering.

'She loved me,' he said. 'She left me there because she loved me. But she was young, and poor, and desperate. She knew she couldn't care for me.'

'Yes,' said Maureen. 'Yes. It could well be true.'

She smiled at us all. But there was the tiredness in her eyes, like she'd heard all of this before. She told us to thank January for sharing so much with us. Then she asked him if he had imagined his father, too. He lowered his eyes. He shook his head.

'No,' he said.

'It may be helpful for your progress,' she said.

She looked at us, as if she wanted us to help January in his task. We said nothing.

'No,' said January. 'He didn't love her. He didn't love me. That's all there is to know.'

His eyes were sullen. She smiled gently. She nodded.

'And she'll come back for me,' he whispered.

'Sorry, dear?'

He stared at her.

'She will. She'll come back for me.'

Fat Kev spat breath. He rolled his eyes.

'She will,' said January. 'She still loves me and wants me. One day she'll come back for me.'

Maureen nodded again. She smiled again. We saw it in her eyes: Damaged, Beyond Repair.

Mouse Gullane is a gentle and timid boy. He wants to

please everyone, so he always tried to play the game. His mother died soon after he was born. His father cared for him for a few years. He showed the photograph of his father playing football with many other men in boiler suits on the banks of the river. Sometimes he pointed to one of the men and said this one was his father. Sometimes it was another of the men. The men in the photograph were so small that he couldn't be certain. He said his father went away because he couldn't care for him.

'He loved me,' he said. 'He must have.'

He showed the blue words his father tattooed on his arm before he went away.

pLeAse LoOk aFter mE.

'See?' he said. 'He was worried about me, even though he knew he was going away.'

Then Mouse just cried and cried.

As for me, I didn't need to play. Maureen said I was stubborn, that if I didn't change, my heart would harden and I'd be filled with bitterness. Once, when I refused to share my memories with her, her eyes glared, her smile disappeared, her voice sharpened. She told me that if I didn't change my ways I'd turn out just like my Mum. And I didn't want that, did I?

'Yes!' I spat at her. 'Yes! Yes!'

I yelled that she knew nothing about my Mum, nothing about her strength and tenderness. I ran out of the room, out of the house, out of the estate. Behind me I heard Maureen at the gate, calling my name, but I took no notice of her. I ran to the river and sat there among the ruins of the past and watched the water flowing towards the sea. I burned with happiness. Despite everything, I burned with happiness. Yes, I know about pain and darkness. Sometimes I go so far into the darkness that I'm scared I'll not get out again. But I do get out, and I do begin to burn again. I don't need to imagine my life. I don't need the stupid circle times. I don't need to build a stupid Life Story book. My head is filled with memories, is always filled with memories. I see my Mum and me in our little house in St Gabriel's Estate. I feel her touch on my skin. I feel her breath on my face. I smell her perfume. I hear her whispering in my ear. I have my little cardboard treasure box, and at any moment I can bring my lovely Mum back to me.

Two

It's easy to run away from Whitegates. Most of us have done it at one time or another. They're always telling us that it's not a prison here, that it's not their job to lock us up. You just sling your sack on your back and stroll out and say you're off for a picnic or something. Mostly we get a few hours of freedom, till hunger or a wet night drives us back again. Sometimes somebody manages a week or more away till they're brought back in a police car, and they wander back inside half-starved, with bags under their eyes, and with a big grin on their face.

My running-away friend was always January Carr. We'd gone off a couple of times together. Once we spent the night across the river in Norton. We bedded down at the back of a restaurant in cardboard boxes, and ate cold pizzas we found in a bin bag there. Another time we wandered right up the riverbank towards the moors and slept on the heather beneath the glittering sky. We saw shooting stars and talked about the universe going on for ever and ever. We talked about wandering for years like this, two vagabonds, free as the beasts and birds, keeping away from the city, drinking from streams, feeding on rabbits and berries. No reason why we couldn't, we whispered to each other. No reason why. We woke next morning with a police dog licking our faces, and a policeman standing there with his hands on his hips, shaking his head.

'Come on,' he said. 'Come on, silly kids.'

We use different methods for getting away. Usually it's just walking. But there's hitch-hiking as well. There's buses and trains. There's cars that can be pinched, and driven till the tank's empty. January's new idea was different, though. Nobody had tried going off on a raft before. Only crazy January could come up with something like that.

He came into my room one morning. He crouched in the doorway, grinning.

'A raft?' I said.

'Aye, a raft. We'll sail away on the river and leave all this behind.'

I laughed. I thought of the dark deep river, the powerful currents, the danger.

'You're mad,' I said.

His eyes were wide and excited.

'It's beautiful,' he said. 'I pinched some doors from one of the old warehouses. I nailed them to planks.' He giggled. 'I've even varnished the bloody thing.'

'You're mad,' I said again. 'It'll sink. We'll drown.'

'Drown! Where's your spirit of adventure?'

I sighed. I could already feel the river running underneath me, pulling me away.

'Imagine it,' he whispered. 'Just me and you and the raft and the river. Freedom, Erin. Freedom.'

I imagined it: the moon shining down on us, the city's lights shining on the banks, the water running through my fingers.

'Wow,' I whispered. 'Wow!'

'Aye,' he said. 'Just imagine, eh?'

Then Maureen shouted from downstairs.

'January! January Carr! I hope that's not you I can hear in Erin's room.

He stood up quietly.

'Just you and me, Erin, sailing away to freedom. Just imagine.'

He winked and tiptoed out.

For weeks afterwards, I felt the river flowing beneath me. I imagined the rocking raft. I dreamed of the journey. I knew I'd go with him.

Three

The Friday we left, we had circle time again. Maureen had this green silky frock on with white shoes and she held a hand against her face and looked fondly at us all. Fat Kev and Skinny Stu were strolling at our backs. Jan kept grinning when I caught his eye.

Maureen gave us the usual rubbish: how this was a safe place, how we all cared for each other, how we could say anything we wanted and it would go no further.

'We want you to be frightened of nothing,' she said. 'We want to heal your scars and wash your cares away.'

She made us do some visualising stuff. We had to imagine we were in a warm dark place, floating in warm dark water. Our minds and bodies were still. There was no future, no past, no trouble. The water that I imagined was icy cold and running fast. Moonlight shining down, the raft spinning and rolling. Freedom. Freedom. I opened my eyes and grinned at Jan and saw the river and the moonlight in his eyes as well. Then Maureen told us to bring our minds into the room again. Straight away she started going on about trouble, about damage, about unhappiness. I looked around at all the faces. I looked at Maxie Ross chewing his fingers and hoping desperately she wouldn't start on him. I looked at Fingers Wyatt, at her beautiful green eyes, at the scalds and burn-marks on her throat. I looked at Wilson Cairns, so fat that his hips spilled down over his chair, who sat motionless, staring blankly at the wall. Wilson. He was one of the few who never tried to run away. He was so fat he could hardly walk, never mind run. He came here carrying a tiny suitcase, a bag of clay and some modelling tools. It was said that he'd almost died at the hands of his parents. Whitegates was a place of safety for him, a place where he could dream, work with his clay, and imagine his own astounding world. Maureen had long since given up trying to get him to talk during circle time. He wore thick bottle-bottom glasses that made his eyes look huge. He hardly spoke at all, even to us. But it wasn't shyness or fear. Behind his glasses, beneath his fat, Wilson roamed the limits of his imagination, and he worked magic with his podgy fingers. When he spoke at all, it was in an effort to make us understand his strange adventures, to make us see his magic. I looked at timid Mouse and at January lounging with his legs splayed, chewing gum, sighing like he was just bored with everything. I looked at everyone and thought of the great times we had together: whispering in somebody's room at midnight, eating nicked sweets and smoking nicked fags and swigging nicked sherry; running riot down by the river in the old warehouses; sitting at dusk in the concrete garden together, whispering our real secrets, speaking our real dreams. We were so different when we were gathered in here like this. It was like Maureen knew nothing about us. Nothing.

'You look anxious today, Sean,' she said.

Sean was the real name of Mouse. He jumped like a scared cat. He blushed, and tears came to his eyes.

'What's troubling you? Would you like to share it with us?'

'N . . . nothing,' he said. 'N . . . n . . . nothing's wrong.'

She leaned forward and smiled.

'Sean. We know all about your troubles. Come on, tell Maureen and your friends. Is it your Dad again?'

Poor Mouse. Such an innocent. I'd told him lots of times: don't tell her the truth. Make something up. Anything. Tell them a pack of lies, Mouse. But he fell for it every time, and there he was again, trembling and sobbing and showing the tattooed words on his arm again while Maureen cooed and pulled the tale out of him and Fat Kev stood behind him scratching his big belly.

'Leave him alone,' I said.

'Pardon?' said Maureen.

'She said leave him alone,' said Skinny Stu from behind me.

Maureen tilted her head and gently clicked her tongue. She composed a smile for me.

'You're angry today, aren't you, Erin?' she said.

'No, I'm not. Just leave him alone.'

I looked through the wide window at the estate outside.

The sun was pouring down. I could just see the river sparkling beyond the red-brick houses and the blocks of flats. I felt the varnished raft beneath my fingers. I tasted sour river water on my tongue. Maureen was watching me.

'You have such a far-away look, Erin,' she said. 'Tell us where you are.'

'Nowhere.'

She clicked her tongue.

'I do wish you'd co-operate,' she said.

'Do you?'

'We're only trying to help you all.'

I shrugged. I smelt the sea on the icy breeze. I closed my eyes. Freedom. Freedom.

'You have to understand,' I heard her say. 'Children like yourselves . . .'

'What do you mean?' I said. 'Children like ourselves?'

I opened my eyes. She looked sadly at me. She sighed.

'You know what I mean, Erin. Children who have difficulties in their lives. Children without the benefits and advantages that others take for granted. Children who will have to struggle always to keep up. Children who through no fault of their own . . .

She dabbed her lips with her handkerchief.

'It gives me no pleasure to say so,' she murmured. 'But you are children who will never be the world's favourites.'

I felt my body rocking on the raft. I stared at all the faces.

'Look at us,' I said. 'There's nothing wrong with us. We can do anything we want to do. Anything.'

Maureen smiled. You could see what she was thinking: Damaged child, wild mind, thinks she can do anything but she'll come to nothing. Nothing. Just like that useless mother of hers.

'We're thinking of your happiness,' she said.

I felt the river spray on my face.

'But I *am* happy,' I murmured.

'Pardon?'

'She says she's happy,' said Skinny Stu.

Maureen pursed her lips. She glared. I saw it in her eyes: How can you be happy? How can you be?

Then she waved her hand bitterly in the air.

'Session over,' she said. 'We'll try again tomorrow when we're all in a better frame of mind.'

We filed out of the room. As I left, Maureen took my arm.

'Erin,' she said.

'What?'

'Why do you oppose me so much? What's wrong with you?'

I clicked my tongue.

'What's wrong with *you*, you mean.'

She pursed her lips.

'You seem so hard sometimes,' she said. 'I don't know how to talk to you.'

'Hard!'

'You can cause a lot of pain.'

'Pain!'

She watched me. Tears shone in her eyes.

'Yes, pain. And you're such a strong bright girl. I used to think that, of all the children here, you'd be the one . . .'

'The one that what?'

She shook her head. She lowered her eyes.

'The one that could help me, I suppose. The one that could help me to help the others . . .'

It was hopeless. Ever since I'd come to Whitegates there'd been something between us, something that filled us both with anger. I turned away from her.

'I always thought . . .' she whispered.

'What?'

'That if I'd had a daughter . . .'

I waited.

'What?' I said.

'That if I'd had a daughter . . . she would be like you, Erin.'

I turned and glared at her.

'That's it, isn't it?' I said. 'If you'd had a daughter, you'd have looked after her better than my Mum did! If you'd had a daughter, she wouldn't have ended up in Whitegates! If you'd had a daughter, you wouldn't have been useless and gone and died like my Mum did! Say it. Go on, say it! You'd have been better than my Mum!'

I ran out of the room. I found January in the pool room.

'This afternoon,' I whispered.

He grinned like a devil.

'This afternoon.'

Four

I went upstairs and started to pack. I pulled the little rucksack from under my bed. I stuffed in some clothes and some food I'd saved for this: cans of Coke, bags of crisps, a packet of biscuits. I put in the knife and torch I'd bought last time we'd run off. I put in some soap and shampoo and a little towel. I counted my money, three pounds twenty-seven. I reached into the back of a drawer and took out my cardboard treasure box.

I loosened the ribbon that was fastened around it and I lifted off the lid. I took out the lock of Mum's hair, her parrot earring, the creased photograph of us in the garden of our little house, the photograph from the hospital that showed me growing inside her, her lipstick, her nail varnish, her final bottle of perfume. I laid these things on my pillow. I put a thin layer of her Sunset lipstick on. I touched the nail varnish – Black Tulip – on to my little fingernail. I tipped up her bottle of Dark Velvet perfume on to my fingertip, then pressed my fingertip to my throat. I lay on my bed in the shadows. A gentle breeze flowed in from an open window. I closed my eyes.

'Mum,' I whispered. 'Mum.'

Nothing.

I breathed deeply, drawing her scent into me.

'Mum!'

I thought of the little house where we'd lived together so happily. I thought of the way she used to laugh, the way we used to play. I remembered how fierce her eyes were when they faced the world and how they filled with tenderness when they turned to me. She'd known so much grief and trouble in her life, but she used to say it didn't matter what had happened in the past and it didn't matter what might happen in the future. Our time together in St Gabriel's would always be her Paradise.

'Mum,' I whispered. 'Mum! Mum!'

I thought of all her stories. The story of how she met my father. She was just a few years older than I am now. He was some waster from a foreign trawler that had come up river to shelter from a storm at sea. He enticed her with a seaman's tales of adventure and charmed her with lies about love. They spent a night together in a cheap bed-and-breakfast place above the quay. She woke next morning all alone. She looked out of the window to see his boat dancing daintily back towards the sea. She said that as she stood there at the window she already felt the new creature – me – trembling and burning with life inside her.

'Mum,' I whispered. 'Mum!'

I breathed deeply. I opened my eyes. I gazed at the

photograph they took at the hospital of me growing inside her. There I was, a tiny thing, swimming, floating in her, waving my arms and kicking my legs. There was the cord that joined me to her. Her food was my food, her blood was my blood. I remembered her stories of how she prepared for me, how she bought my cot from Oxfam, how she stuck pictures of angels and fairies on the wall of the bedroom we were to share, how her excitement grew as I grew inside her, as her Paradise approached. She used to hold her belly gently. She already whispered my name: Erin, Erin. She already sang songs to me, and told me how wonderful it would be when I was born and we were together in the world.

'Mum,' I whispered. 'Mum.'

I pictured her brilliant green eyes, her red hair that grew like fire around her pretty face. I saw her parrot earrings dangling. I saw her brightly coloured lips, her glistening dark fingernails. I imagined her touch, her voice. I remembered the days in St Gabriel's, how we were as much like best friends as like mother and daughter. We were so happy. We needed no one else. But sometimes we did talk of what might happen if she met a good man. We did talk of the other children that might come along – my brothers, my sisters. Would you like that? she used to ask me, and I used to answer, Yes. Oh, yes. And in my dreams I saw them, those brothers and sisters, so tender and so lovely and so filled with joy.

'Mum. Mum.'

I remembered her in the hospital. I was ten, only ten. They

gave her higher and higher doses of morphine to blot out the pain. She moved in and out of reality and dreams. I remembered how she leaned from the bed towards me and cradled my face in her hands. She whispered that she couldn't help herself. She felt as if she was being carried away on water. She told me not to cry. She said she'd be with me always. Always. I held her hand and it grew colder, colder, colder.

'Mum. Mum!'

And at last she came, and she whispered, 'Erin. Erin.'

I felt her hand on my shoulder, her breath on my cheek. I heard the smile in her voice. I felt her arm around me. She cradled me like she did when I was small. I lay against her.

'I love you,' I whispered.

'I know that. And I love you, Erin. I'll always love you. Always.'

'I'm going away on January's raft.'

She giggled.

'I know.'

'And you'll be with me?'

'I'll be with you always, Erin.'

We lay there for a time. I was no longer in Whitegates. We were together in our little garden outside our little house at the edge of St Gabriel's Estate. The garden was filled with bright flowers and fattening gooseberries. Seagulls were screaming above the river that flowed below. I held Mum's hand. She gently sang *Bobby Shaftoe* into my ear. She pressed little mints into my hand. Then she touched my brow with her lips and we were back in Whitegates, in my little room. We lay there. I knew she'd leave me soon. I dreamed of the raft, the river, of floating away. Would I ever come back again?

We smiled when the bird came in. It perched on the frame of the open window for a second, nodding its head as it looked in at us. Then it flew into the room. It was a small dark bird with quick wings, a curious sparrow on its way back to its nest. It flickered over our heads. It circled the room several times.

'A bird!' I said. 'Look! A bird!'

We laughed.

Then it went back to the window, perched, looked back for a second and launched itself into the air above the estate.

I sat up straight and followed it with my eyes.

We laughed again.

'Funny thing,' I said.

'The bird of life,' she said.

'Bird of life?'

'We come into the world out of the dark. We haven't got a clue where we've come from. We've got no idea where we're going. But while we're here in the world, if we're brave enough, we flap our wings and fly.'

I thought about this.

'You understand?' she said.

'I think so.'

She smiled, and just whispered my name time and again.

'Will it come back again?' I asked.

'Who knows? Maybe now it's found this place it'll come back time and again.'

We heard the noise of children in the house.

'Go on, Erin. Go on down. January'll be waiting.'

'You'll be with me?'

'I'll be with you. Go on. Don't stay here in the shadows with me. Flap your wings. Fly away.'

Then she was gone, and there was just the sound of a television on the floor below, and somebody sobbing upstairs. I gently put my treasures back into their box. I tied the ribbon. I put the box into the rucksack, took a deep breath and went down to find January.

Five

I burst out laughing when I saw him. He was wearing his running-away clothes: black jeans and a black fleece, black trainers with a red flash on them, a black skull hat. He was in the pool room, playing with Hairy Smart. His sack was leaning against the skirting board. He winked and potted a last ball and told Hairy he'd have to stop. Everybody could tell what was going on. Hairy grinned and winked. Fingers slipped to my side.

'You will come back?' she whispered. 'Won't you?'

We gave each other a quick cuddle.

'Course we will,' I said. 'They won't let us get far before they find us and bring us back again.'

I grinned, but I wondered. How will they bring us back from the bottom of the river or the bottom of the sea?

Wilson Cairns sat facing the wall. He was at a little table, working with his clay again. It was his obsession. He did it every day. Maureen said it was helpful for him, it let him recreate some of the childhood he had lost. He had a big ball of the stuff and a basin of water. His hands and the table top were filthy. He had made a little group of muddy people. He held one of them up to his eyes and breathed over it. Then he walked it across the table top. I touched his shoulder and said we'd see him soon.

'It is possible,' he said.

He didn't move except to keep the figure lumbering across the table top.

'Sorry?' I said.

He turned his head as he walked the muddy figure. He stared through the thick glasses. He didn't blink.

'It *is* possible,' he whispered.

He took his hand away from the clay figure and it stood there.

He stared at it.

'Did you see it move?' he whispered.

I stared.

'No.'

He looked at me again, as if he looked right through me to something astonishing behind me.

'You have to keep watching, closely, closely. Or you'll miss it.'

'I will,' I said. 'I'll keep watching.'

I was about to turn away from him.

'I listened to you,' he said.

'Eh?'

'To you. You said we can do anything we want to.'

'Yes.'

'I know that. I know that as well. We can do anything.'

His eyes changed. They focused on me. It was so rare for him to focus clearly on any of us, so rare for him to speak like this to any of us. His fingers ran across the clay figure.

'Anything,' he said. 'Even me. Me, here, facing the wall playing with clay and water. I can do anything.'

I touched his head again.

'Yes. I know that.'

'Even me. Even me, Wilson Cairns. Thick fat ugly Wilson Cairns.'

I smiled.

'You're lovely, Wilson,' I said.

'You'll come back,' he said.

'Yes.'

'I'll watch for you, Erin Law. I'll keep thinking of you.'

He caught his breath.

'Did you see?' he hissed.

'What?'

He held the figure. He gazed down at it and breathed over it. Did I see it move? Did I see a clay arm reach out as if it was alive? Did I see the figure lean forward as if to step away from Wilson? Or was it just the way the light fell on it, the way Wilson's hand trembled? Was it just because I wanted to see?

'I'm not sure,' I said.

He peered through his thick distorting glasses.

'You will,' he said. 'I'll watch for you coming back. It's easy to go away. The magic thing is to come back again.'

I touched his head. I bent down and smiled at him.

'I'll see you soon, lovely Wilson Cairns.'

'Keep watching,' he whispered.

'I will. I'll keep watching.'

'Good. Then come back and watch again.'

I moved away from him and went to January. Fat Kev came into the doorway.

'Hope you two's not planning somethin,' he said.

'As if we would,' I said.

'As if we would,' said Jan.

Kev swiped his fist across his nose and shook his head. He shrugged. It wouldn't matter to him what any of us did, as long as he didn't have to lumber after us, and as long as he got his pay and his big free dinners. I looked at him and giggled, at the thought of the way his belly squashed against the table, the way he snuffled as he shoved the food in. He stared back with his piggy eyes.

'Little madam,' he said, and I thought of the way he was with the scared ones, the way he pushed his face so close to theirs, the way he said he knew ways to fix them if they didn't learn any manners.

'Pig,' I whispered.

'What did you say?'

'Nothing.'

He turned his face away and muttered some filth about me and went out again.

'Pig,' I breathed. 'Pig, pig, pig.'

I kissed Maxie Ross and then Jan and I headed out. Skinny Stu was leaning on the house wall, hiding a fag in his fist. He had his shirt open and his skinny ribcage glared in the late afternoon sun. He shoved his greasy hair back.

'Oh, aye?' he said.

'Aye,' said January. 'We're off for a little picnic.'

'Be back for supper, Stu,' I said.

Stu flicked his ash. He pointed into the sky.

'Hey, you see that?'

'What?' said January.

Stu laughed his dry rattly laugh.

'That flying pig there, son.'

He took a drag.

'See you for supper, then,' he said.

We went through the iron gate. I turned and looked back as we went through the iron gate. I wanted to see Maureen watching us. I wanted to see her weeping as we left. But there was only Wilson. He watched from the pool room, leaning close to the panes, staring at us through his glasses, or at something far beyond us. The sun was falling towards the rooftops. We headed through the estate. We came to the street above the river where I'd lived with Mum. We passed by our house. The garden was all overgrown. The front door was covered in scratches from a dog or something. Music was screeching from inside. I turned my eyes away and we hurried on. On the other side of the river, the city roared. The bridges gleamed in the sunlight. The river glistened. We moved into the waste ground outside St Gabriel's where all the warehouses and terraced streets had been knocked down.

January clenched his fists and thumped the air. I kicked the ground and sent dust dancing around us.

'Freedom!' we shouted. 'Freedom!'

We started running and skipping down towards the river. Then we heard Mouse Gullane.

'Erin! January! What you doing? Where you going?'

Six

He was sitting on an old kerbstone, digging in the dirt with a battered spoon.

January cursed.

'Not him,' he said. 'Come on. Take no notice.'

Mouse jumped to his feet.

'Erin! January!'

He came running towards us. His hands were filthy from his digging. His face was all smudged. Squeak was balancing on his shoulder.

'Look what I found, Erin,' said Mouse.

It was a little blue plastic dinosaur.

'And this,' he said.

He pulled a tiny toy car from his pocket. No wheels, dried dirt clogging the inside, the paint all flaked away.

'And money!' he grinned, showing a five-pence piece.

'Great,' I said. 'They're lovely, Mouse.'

He was always digging for things, collecting things. His room was filled with his discoveries, cleaned up and laid out on his shelves and floor. He said the earth was filled with objects from the past and that one day he'd find real treasure, something really precious in the cold dark earth.

January cursed.

'Come on,' he said.

'Take me with you,' said Mouse. 'I know you're going away.'

'We can't,' I said.

'Please, Erin.'

'It's dangerous. We're going on the river. We might bloody drown.

'Please, Erin.'

January tugged my arm. He cursed again.

'Get lost!' he hissed at Mouse. 'Come on, Erin.'

We turned away and continued heading down. Mouse followed, close behind. We walked over great piles of rubble, all that was left of the warehouses and workplaces. We walked over cinders and blackened earth where kids' bonfires had been. The ground was ruined, cracked, potholed. Crows hopped across the debris. A rat scuttled across our path. There was barbed wire. There were signs telling us to keep out. We scrambled across the fences and kept on walking. 'This way,' Jan kept saying. 'This way. This way.' We walked quickly. We swaggered and swung our arms. Soon, we had left Mouse behind. We picked up half-bricks and bits of broken concrete and slung them high into the air and heard them crashing down again. The sun sank further. The distant moors were outlined darkly against the sky. We could hear the river now, a hundred yards away. It splashed and gurgled against the ancient quays. It caught the falling sunlight. It was like hammered metal, gleaming, with long slow swells that surged towards the distant sea.

'This one,' said Jan at last.

He crouched at a pile of broken bricks and splintered timbers. He started pulling the bricks and timber away.

'Come on,' he said, and I started digging, too.

'There she is,' he whispered.

We saw the corner of a door, the raft's edge. January giggled.

'Come on, my beauty,' he said.

We dug. We threw the rubble aside. We lifted the edge of the raft and tipped it so that the last of the rubble just fell away. Then we hauled the raft free and let it fall with a crash to the earth.

January laughed with joy. He brushed away the dust with his hands.

'Isn't she beautiful, Erin?'

The raft was made of three doors laid flat and nailed down on to planks. On the doors were written the words, in cracked gilt lettering:

ENTRANCE DANGER EXIT

Right across the raft, January had painted a curse in red:

MAy anyWOn whO StEEls thiS rAFT be FerrYD StRAte to HELL!

'Isn't she beautiful?' he said.

'Yes, I said. I turned my head to the darkening water. 'Yes, she is.'

Seven

There was a long tethering rope fastened to one corner. There were two paddles carved from window frames. We carried the paddles across our shoulders. We hauled the raft across the broken ground. From somewhere in the ruins, kids appeared. They stood on the heaps and watched. The raft squeaked and cracked as we dragged. The sun fell. My heart thundered. We came to the quays and looked down at the churning filthy river.

'Hell's teeth,' I said.

January grinned.

'Scared?' he asked.

'No. Petrified.'

He giggled.

'We just drop it, then we jump. Then we go. Easy.'

'What if it sinks?'

'You can swim?'

'Yes.'

'Well, then.'

'Hell's teeth, January.'

His eyes were devilish.

'Hell's teeth, Erin.'

He laughed. He kicked the raft.

'Look at it. Solid as a rock. This thing won't sink.'

I didn't know if I could do it. I looked down river, saw the mist rising as evening approached.

'We could just walk,' I said.

'Walk! Where's your spirit of adventure?'

We crouched close together. He stared into my eyes.

'What we got to lose?' he said.

My life, I thought.

'Nothing,' I said.

'And we've got each other. We'll be in this together.'

'Yes.'

'Well, then.'

I took deep breaths.

'OK,' I whispered.

Then Mouse was beside us.

'Take me,' he said.

'Go home,' said January.

Mouse pulled his sleeve back. He showed us his tattoo.

pLeAse LoOk aFter mE.

'Please,' he said.

I looked at Jan.

'Hell's teeth, Erin,' he said.

'Can you swim?' I asked.

Mouse shook his head.

'Please, Erin. Please.'

'Jan,' I said. 'What d'you think?'

He cursed. He spat.

'Hell's bloody teeth,' he hissed.

He grabbed Mouse by the collar.

'What you brought?' he said.

'Brought?'

'Food. Money. Clothes. A knife.'

Mouse showed the dinosaur, the car, the five-pence piece. He took out the cracked photograph of the men in boiler suits from his back pocket. He held Squeak in his loosely closed fist.

'Eek,' said Squeak. 'Eek, eek!'

'Fantastic,' said Jan. 'These'll all come in very handy when the going gets tough.'

He shoved Mouse.

'Go home,' he said. 'You'll just be in time for one of Kev's ghost stories.'

'Home?' said Mouse. 'I've got no home. I'm just like you. I've got nowhere. I can go anywhere. Please.

'You'll drown,' said January.

'I don't care. I don't blooming care. Please. Please.'

He held out the five-pence piece.

'I'll pay you,' he said.

'Pay!' laughed January.

'Go on,' said Mouse. 'Take it. Please. It'll be my fare. Take it and take me with you.'

Dusk was coming. The sun was a huge orange ball sliding

down behind the moors. The sky over the city was starting to burn. The mist down river thickened. We stood there on the quay in silence, lost in our thoughts.

'The raft's big enough,' I whispered. 'Three people. Three doors.'

I touched January's arm.

'I'll look after him,' I said.

'Hell's teeth, Erin,' he said.

Then he shrugged. He took Mouse's five-pence piece and grinned. He stooped to the raft again.

'Come on,' he said. 'Let's do it. All aboard.'

We slid the raft over the edge. It balanced there, then crashed down into the water. Jan held on to the tethering rope. The raft disappeared while the water seethed above it. Stay down, I thought. Don't come up again. Then it rose and rested bobbing on the water.

Jan grinned and squeezed my arm.

'Go on,' he said.

He laughed at Mouse.

'Go on. Go on. You as well. All aboard.'

Eight

Was it the scariest moment of my life? No. That was the moment when Mum closed her eyes for the final time and left me all alone. But my head reeled. My heart thudded. My legs trembled. As I stepped over the edge and climbed down the rotting timbers of the quay, I thought I was climbing down to my death. Mouse climbed beside me. He gave me strength. 'Come on,' he whispered. 'Come on, Erin.' January watched us from above. He hauled back on the tethering rope, keeping the raft close to the quay. But there was still a three-feet gap between us and the edge.

'Jump!' yelled January. 'Go on. Jump!'

Mouse went first. He landed face down in the centre, with his feet dangling back into the water. He laughed. He turned.

'Come on, Erin!' he called.

'Mum,' I whispered. 'Mum. Mum!'

I closed my eyes and leapt. I skidded on the varnish, on the water that was slopping across the doors. I squatted at the centre with Mouse. Jan threw the paddles down. Then there was a scream and he came hurtling down on top of us. The raft lurched, slewed sideways, was caught by the current, and we were dragged away.

We goggled at each other. We gasped and yelled with terror and excitement. The raft spun out towards the centre of the river. The sky was vivid red. The river was like running molten metal. The massive bridge arched over us. We were drenched in seconds. We clung to each other. The water quickened, dragging us down towards the thickening mist. Suddenly January leapt up. He stretched his arms towards the sky.

'AAAAAHHH!' he yelled. 'AAAAHHH! FREEDOM!'

The raft rocked and toppled him back on to us again.

His eyes were wild with joy. His face burned like the sky.

'Freedom,' he whispered. 'Freedom, Erin!

Nine

There were eddies and swirling currents. There were little waves whipped up by the breeze. The river didn't take one single course. We were dragged out to the centre then back towards the bank. We tried to control the raft with the paddles but they were skinny things, almost useless. At one time we were dragged upstream and it seemed we'd be heading to the distant moors rather than towards the distant sea. But then the current turned again and took us down again. We were bitter cold. We were sodden. Soon it was like the river had soaked through to our bones. All the time the evening darkened, darkened. The city started to glare: brilliant lights outside the pubs and clubs on Norton Quay. Music echoed across the water. We saw the people gathering there in bright skimpy clothes, out for the night. A group of girls pointed out to us. They danced a jig and yelled out *Bobby Shaftoe*. Others watched, serious, maybe worried about us. Jan yelled *Bobby Shaftoe* back at them. 'Nice night for a paddle!' he called. The girls squealed. The river dragged us towards them, then spun us back into the centre again. We waved, trying to reassure the worried ones, trying to reassure ourselves. 'Hell's teeth,' Jan kept saying. 'Hell's teeth,' I answered. 'Hell's teeth,' whispered Mouse. He held me tight, wouldn't let go. His teeth were chattering, his voice was quivering. 'It's going to be all right!' he said. 'It is! It's going to be all right.' Tears poured from his eyes. 'Erin!' he yelled in terror. 'Erin!' We plunged onwards. We seemed to catch the main current and it drew us relentlessly away from the lights, away from the voices, towards the mist, towards the night. The moon appeared, a white ball that brightened as the sky around it deepened into black. Stars glittered, first a handful then a skyful. We passed the city's dark outskirts, the dilapidated quays: more ruined warehouses, broken wharves, massive billboards showing how this place would be once the demolishing, building and developing started. Huge gaps of blackness where there was nothing. The river stank of oil and something rotten. There was the scent of salt and seaweed. We passed the stream called the Ouseburn and hit more eddies where the currents of the stream and river mixed. Then the mist, thin at first, still allowing the moon and stars through to us. But it thickened, deepened. Soon there was nothing but us, the raft, the churning water and the mist. Our voices boomed and echoed back to us. We stared at each other, held each other, in terror that one of us might be lost to the others, in terror that we'd all be lost, in terror that this journey was nothing but a journey into death. We muttered bits of prayers, we called out for help, we forgot about the paddles and we drifted, rocked, lurched and spun. And then we slowed and the raft jerked, shuddered, and we stopped. Just water gently slopping, the gentle creaking of the doors beneath us. Just the gasping of our breath. And silence all around.

PART TWO

THE BLACK MIDDENS

One

Mud. Black, sticky, oily, stinking mud. It was January who dared to lean out of the raft first. He dipped his hand into what should have been water. He touched mud, black mud. It oozed and dribbled from his fingers. The raft settled, and mud slithered across its surface, on to our clothes. It seeped through to our skin. It seeped through the tiny gaps between the doors. I took my torch out, switched it on, saw the doors disappearing as they sank, saw the gilt words and the red curse obscured, saw the mud rise, saw that we were being slowly sucked down into the sodden earth. 'Hell's teeth,' we hissed. 'Hell's teeth.' We crawled to each other, clutched each other. Our feet, our heels, our knees were caught in mud.

'The Black Middens,' said January.

'What?'

'The Black Middens. We're grounded on the bloody Black Middens.'

I shone the torch into his eyes.

'Got to get out,' he said. 'It'll suck us in.'

We leaned out, tried to shove ourselves free. The raft just sank deeper.

'Hell's teeth,' I hissed.

I shone the torch into the mist. Water behind us, black mud in front, impenetrable mist.

'There'll be dry land further in,' said January.

We reached across the mud, searching for this dry land. Just mud. Wet black lethal mud. We goggled at each other. We gasped and sobbed in fright.

'Somebody'll have to go, Erin. Somebody'll have to take the rope and get to the dry land.'

We stared into each other's eyes.

'Me,' said Mouse.

I didn't turn.

'You can't even swim,' I whispered.

'You're lighter than me,' said January.

'I know I am.'

I put the torch between my teeth. I took the end of the rope. I slid across the edge of the raft. I stretched my arms and legs wide. I crawled. I kept moving. I slithered forward. I felt how at any moment I could stop and be taken down into The Black Middens. I whispered for my Mum. There was no answer. Mouse and January spoke my name from behind. I couldn't speak. I grunted, whimpered, groaned. I slithered forward. There was no dry land, no dry land. My head filled with the mist and darkness. I cried. At one point I just stopped moving. I told myself that this is what I had come out on the raft for. I was following my Mum down river. She waited for me deep in The Black Middens. I began to let myself be taken down. I felt the mud gathering around me. I felt the great contentment that might come if I just let go, if I sank here, if I just let myself go down to her, if my mouth was filled with mud, if my eyes and ears were filled with mud, if there was nothing but mud surrounding me, encasing me.

And then I heard her: 'Erin. Erin.' I felt her hands holding me, preventing me from sinking. 'Erin,' she whispered. 'Keep moving. Don't let go.' She helped me drag my body free. She held me up as I continued. I stretched forward as I slithered and crawled. And at last I touched drier, firmer ground. I hauled myself on to it. I knelt there and sobbed and couldn't speak. The others called for me. I heard the terror in their voices. I pulled on the rope. It tightened. 'It's all right,' I called. 'I'm all right.' I told them to come after me, to follow the rope. And when they gripped the rope and hauled themselves, they too slithered through the mud and darkness. We shone our torches on to each other. We were black glistening trembling things, like creatures formed from water, earth and blackness a million million years ago. We clutched each other, held each other tight. An age might have passed before we came out of our horror and released each other. Then January spat and cursed.

'The bloody raft,' he said. 'Got to drag it in.'

He glared at us.

'Didn't make it to lose it on the first bloody trip. And didn't make it to get no further than the bloody Black Middens.'

So we pulled on the rope. We grunted and cursed. We slowly slowly dragged the raft back to us. We hauled it on to the dry land. We lay there, exhausted.

Then I felt her hand on my shoulder. I heard her voice. I turned and saw her face for the first time, her pale beseeching eyes gazing into mine.

'Is you my sister?' she asked. 'Is these mine brothers?'

Two

There were webs stretched between her fingers. Her face was moon-pale. Her eyes were moon-round, watery-blue. Her voice was high and light and yearning.

'Is you? Is you?' she said.

Mouse squealed. January gripped his knife in his fist. We backed away. We stepped back into the black wetness. She reached out to us.

'Do not go back into them Middens, my long-lost sister, my long-lost brothers.'

We felt the mud sucking us into itself.

She wept.

'Do not go back again!'

'Oh, hell,' sobbed Mouse. 'Oh, hell. Oh, hell.'

I slithered back to the dry land. Mouse and January slithered back. We crouched together. January and I shone our torches on to her.

'You must come with me,' she said.

She rested her webbed fingers on my arm again.

She sighed.

'What is your name?' she said.

'Erin.'

'Ah. Such lovely naming of a sister.'

She beamed with delight.

'I has waited that long, Erin. Now you must come with me to Grampa. I did tell him I did see you. Now you must come and show yourself to him.'

We didn't move. Mist flowed through the torch beams.

'He is waiting,' she said.

'Who?' said January.

'Grampa. My Grampa. Look.'

She turned and the mist lightened. The torch beams showed the figure behind her, watching. He was tall, black as the night and the mud. He wore shorts and heavy boots. He carried a bucket in one hand, a huge shovel in the other.

'Here they is, Grampa!' she called. 'Didn't me tell you? Here is my treasures come out of the black Black Middens.'

His eyes glittered as he watched us. He coughed and spat.

'Push them back into the runny water, my little one,' he said.

'Oh, Grampa!'

He took a step towards us with his shovel raised.

'Let me dig them back into the mud,' he said.

'Oh, Grampa!'

He stood still and watched her.

'They are nothing to you,' he said.

'Grampa. Mebbe true these is my treasures come at last.'

He clawed mud from his face, threw it back down on to

the Middens. The fog rolled back across him.

'Bring them to me,' he said. 'And we will see what we will see.'

We heard him turn and his feet sucked and slopped as he stepped away.

'I will bring them to you, Grampa,' she said. 'Go and clean yourself and I will bring them to you.'

She held out her hands to us.

'Come,' she said.

We didn't move.

'There is warmness and comfort and food,' she said.

'He'll bloody kill us,' said Jan.

'No,' she said. 'He will love you and look after you like he loves Heaven Eyes and looks after Heaven Eyes.'

'You are Heaven Eyes?' I said.

'I is Heaven Eyes, my sister.'

She beamed.

'You must come,' she said. 'There is danger on these Middens. You must come before the runny water comes again and washes us away.

I looked at January, at Mouse. There was nothing we could do.

'Come, come,' she sang.

She led us across the dry land. We dragged the raft behind us. We tied it to an ancient tethering ring. We followed her up an ancient ladder to the ancient quay. As she climbed, I saw that there were webs between her toes. At the top, she took our hands and helped us up. She reached out to our faces. Each of us recoiled. She smiled.

'Do not be feared, my sister and brothers,' she said. 'There is nothing here to make you feared.'

She reached out again to January and Mouse.

'And who is you?' she said. 'And who is you?'

'This is January Carr,' I said. 'This is Mouse Gullane. I am Erin Law.'

'Oh,' she sang. 'Such lovely lovelies. Come. Come and follow Heaven Eyes!'

Three

As we stepped up on to the quay, we stepped out of the mist. There were teetering warehouses, collapsed walls, dark alleyways. Rafters and smashed rooftops were outlined against the sky. There were great cracks and potholes in the ground. Mud and water drained from us, splashed from us.

Heaven Eyes beckoned us. She turned into an alleyway, plunged into the deep shadow there.

'Follow,' she said. 'Follow. Follow.'

She led us through a tangle of alleyways and lanes. Her pale hair bobbed and streamed before us. Often she turned and her eyes shone as she waited for us to catch up. Her voice sang out the single word: Follow, follow, follow. We bumped into walls and trod in potholes. We skinned our knuckles on the stone. We twisted and turned, ducked through low entrances. We walked across the crumbling floors of dilapidated buildings. By the light of the moon we saw the red signs telling of danger. There were drawings of guards and snarling guard dogs. Everywhere the signs said, KEEP OUT, **KEEP OUT**, ***KEEP OUT!*** We followed

Heaven Eyes, her thin legs, her pale hair, her shining eyes, her song-like voice. Follow, follow, follow, follow.

We entered a huge building. Moonlight poured in wedges through the shattered skylights. There were great dark machines with statues of eagles and angels squatting above them. The floor was a litter of rubble, paper, broken glass. There were great toppling heaps of books, newspapers, magazines.

She stopped, beneath a huge black pair of outspread wings.

'This is where books was made,' she said. 'See?'

She stooped down and picked a handful of metal letters from among the litter at her feet.

'See?' she said.

She opened her hand and they rattled back on to the floor.

'But way way time back,' she said.

She smiled and her eyes gleamed.

'Grampa is the caretaker,' she said. 'Is in there, look.'

She turned her head towards a boarded-up window. Tiny chinks of light shone between the boards. On the door beside the window was a white sign:

C RET KER

'He is waiting,' she said. 'He will be ready for you now.'

January and I stared at each other. January gripped his knife again.

'Come now,' she said. 'Come all of you.'

She turned the door handle and stepped inside.

'Here they is, Grampa,' she sang. 'And oh they is so wet and cold and oh so feared.'

Grampa sat hunched forward at a table in the middle of the office. He was writing in a huge thick book. Candles burned on the table and on the shelves that lined the walls. A little fire glowed in a tiny grate. He turned his face to us as we stood in the threshold behind Heaven Eyes. Long straggling black hair, a black beard, black sediment in the creases that filled his face. His watery eyes sparkled in the candlelight as he gazed at us in turn. He now wore a black jacket, with epaulettes. The word SECURITY was written on his chest pocket. There was a black peaked helmet on the table beside him.

'This is Grampa,' said Heaven Eyes. 'And Grampa, this is Erin Law, Janry Carr and Mouse Gullane. These is lovely names for a lovely sister and lovely brothers.'

He turned his eyes to Heaven, but said nothing.

'Come in,' she said. She rested her webbed fingers on my arm. 'Come in and close the night away.'

She leaned past me and closed the door behind us.

'Here is comfort, and food to eat and drink to drink.'

She held out a stone jar filled with water.

'Drink,' she said. 'Wash out the Middens from your mouths. Then eat. We has sultanas and corned beef and many chocolates.'

She drew me towards the fire. She knelt and showed me the bucket there. She dipped her hands in and washed them. The webs were pale and the light of the fire glowed through them.

She giggled.

'You is all filthy as filthy, Erin Law.'

She stroked my hands with her wet fingers.

'Wash like me,' she said. 'Wash away the Middens, Erin Law.'

She bit her lips as I knelt beside her and my shoulders touched hers.

'Oh, Erin,' she whispered. 'Oh, Erin my sister.'

Behind us, January and Mouse were stock-still, their eyes fixed on Grampa. He stared back, then began scribbling again in his great book.

'Children, three,' he muttered as he wrote. 'Brought out from the Middens. Boys, two. Girls, one. Cold, filthy, dirty and afraid. Mebbe they're ghosts. Mebbe they're devils sent from hell or angels sent from heaven. More likely something in between, come to do shenanigans. Push them back, Grampa. Dig them back in. Do it.' He stabbed the page with his pencil point then paused, with his pencil poised above the page. He jutted his face towards us all. He inspected us. 'You are not the brothers,' he said. 'You are not the sister.'

I shook my head. I met his gaze.

'We never said we were,' I told him.

His face hardened as he stared, then softened as he smiled at Heaven Eyes.

'It is a wrongness in you, little one,' he said.

'A wrongness?'

'These are not your brothers. This is not your sister.'

'No?'

'No, my lovely. You were wrong. So mebbe we must put them back into the Black Middens where you found them.'

'We came from the river on a raft,' I said. 'We didn't come out of the Black Middens.'

'And you is not my sister?' said Heaven Eyes.

Her eyes beseeched me. I gazed at her. Did she look like me? Was there anything in her that looked like me? Could she be my sister? Could we share a father? I lowered my eyes. I knew that if I had ever written my Life Story book, I would have imagined sisters and brothers for myself. I would have found them in my dreams. But this was all wrong, as Grampa had said. I shook my head and put my thoughts aside.

'No,' I said. 'I am not your sister. These are not your brothers. Each of us is all alone.'

She closed her eyes.

'It was a wrongness, then,' she whispered. 'It was all just wanting and imagining.'

She stared at us.

'You is ghosts?'

'No. We're not ghosts,' I answered.

'Good,' she said. 'For there is many ghosts sometimes.'

Then she smiled again.

'You might not be my sister,' she said. 'But Erin Law, you could be my bestest friend.'

She watched me.

'Yes?' she whispered.

I touched her cool smooth cheek. I looked deep into her

eyes. Yes, I thought. Yes, a friend who is almost a sister.

'Yes,' I said. 'Yes.'

'My Grampa,' she said.

'Yes, my little one.'

Her eyes filled with tears as she spoke to him.

'Do not push them back into the runny water. Do not dig them back into the Middens. Let them stay with you and me.'

'This will make you happy?' said Grampa.

'Yes. Yes. For I has never had a friend like Erin Law.'

Grampa sighed and groaned and gazed darkly at us as he nodded in reply.

'Yes,' he murmured.

Heaven squeezed me. She beamed at January and Mouse.

'See,' she said. 'He is a good Grampa. He will take care of you as he has taken care of Heaven Eyes.'

He turned his eyes to the page again.

'Names. They have names, so fast forgotten.'

He scratched his beard and black dust fell from it to his page.

'Come on, Grampa,' he said. 'Names, three.'

'Erin Law, Janry Carr and Mouse Gullane,' said Heaven Eyes. 'He is old and does not memory much. He writes all down.'

'Erin, Janry and Mouse,' he whispered as he wrote.

'This is good,' said Heaven. 'He is putting you inside his book and in the tale of Heaven Eyes and Grampa and the black Black Middens.'

'What is the tale?' I said.

'Oh, is a dark and wet and filthy tale.'

'You'll tell me it?'

'Mebbe, Erin. But even Heaven Eyes does not know a way to tell it true.'

She held my face.

'Erin Law. Heaven Eyes has never had a bestest friend.'

She swayed her shoulders and head and hummed a tune. I sighed and smiled and looked at January. He curled his lip and cursed. His eyes were cold.

'What's wrong?' I hissed.

He just turned his face away.

Heaven Eyes touched his shoulder.

'Come,' she said. 'Come and wash away the black Black Middens.'

He shrugged her off, but he knelt with Mouse at the bucket and they washed their hands and faces there.

Heaven Eyes went to Grampa and kissed his cheek.

'These is nice children,' she told him. 'Mebbe it was wrong to say these is my sister and my brothers. But they is certainly not ghosts. And now Heaven will look after them and make them not so feared.'

She picked a box up from the floor.

'There is sultanas and beef,' she said. 'And there is many of the sweetest chocolates.'

She opened the lid of the box and held it out to us. We took chocolates. We took more chocolates. She held out an opened tin of Fray Bentos corned beef.

'Take more,' she said. 'Take more. Be not feared. Take the thing that looks the nicest thing of all.'

Four

'There must be places for the night,' said Heaven Eyes. 'There must be places for the sleeping and the sleep thoughts.'

She laid blankets in a row against the wall.

'For you all,' she whispered. 'For you to be fast asleep and safe and sound in Grampa's office.'

Mouse crouched beside her as she worked. He picked up metal letters from the floor and laid out our names beside our blankets.

ERin
JanRy
MoWs & skweEk

'What is these letters?' said Heaven Eyes.

'Our names,' he said.

He spoke the letters, spelling out the words.

'See?' he said. 'The letters make words and words make us.'

She pondered.

'Is there letters that make Heaven Eyes?'

Mouse smiled, and laid her own name there beside her blankets.

hEvan ayES

She smiled, and gently touched her letters.

'Is me?' she said.

'It's you,' said Mouse.

'Lovely. Lovely.'

She wriggled down on to her blankets with her hand stretched out to touch her name.

January kicked his own letters away.

'Like a name on a bloody gravestone,' he said.

I clicked my tongue.

Heaven Eyes lay beside me beneath her own blankets.

'My bestest friend,' she said.

She rested her head on my arm and slept.

Mouse went off to sleep quickly and peacefully, as if nothing here troubled him.

January and I lay on our blankets, rested our heads on our hands and looked at each other. Jan's eyes were harsh and red-rimmed and shining with tiredness. I saw how he was ready to quarrel with me, even to fight with me. I tasted the sweetness of the chocolates in my mouth, the juice of the sultanas, felt the heaviness of the cold meat in my stomach. Heaven's voice echoed deep inside my mind. I felt the touch of her webbed fingers on my cheek. The little fire's gentle heat drifted over us. I felt the Middens mud drying on me, encasing me.

'It's warm,' I said. 'We're tired, Jan. We have to stay, at least for tonight.'

He glanced at Grampa, who stayed sitting at the table, taking no notice of us. He kept on writing, writing. He muttered and whispered as he wrote. Black dust fell from his hair and beard to the page.

'They're mad,' said January. 'They're bloody freaks.'

'They won't harm us.'

'Like something from a bloody nightmare. Look at him. No knowing what he'll do . . .'

'But she's lovely.'

'Lovely!'

'Yes, lovely. Old as us, but like a little girl. And so strange, Jan . . .'

He shook his head and ground his teeth.

'A freak, you mean. A mutant. Like something from a stupid zoo.'

'Stop it!'

He narrowed his eyes.

'You're under a spell, Erin. All that stuff about brothers and sisters and bestest friends!'

'A spell ! Ha!'

Grampa grunted. He looked down at us.

'Not brother,' he said. 'Not sister.'

I shook my head at him.

'No,' I said. 'We know that, Grampa.'

'We know that, Grampa,' echoed January in a little

mocking voice, then he lowered his head, turned his back to me. Soon his breathing slowed and deepened. Grampa turned back to his book.

Five

Behind Grampa, the shelves on the wall were packed. I could make out broken bits of pottery, heaps of coins, rusted knives and tools. There were rows of bottles and metal boxes. There was a small boat's propeller and a little anchor. There was a little stack of bleached bones. On the highest shelves, right up against the ceiling, there were boxes lashed tight with belts and ropes. Three spades leaned on the wall beside the door. There were several buckets, one inside the other. Grampa murmured and wrote. Heaven Eyes slept on my arm. Sometimes she hummed as she slept and it was like music that came from a thousand miles away. I rubbed my eyes to keep myself from sleep and dreams.

Grampa's hands were like ours, grainy and black. Black dust as well as scribbled words fell from his fingers. He kept staring into the darkness, pondering, tapping on his table.

'Tuesday,' he said. 'Unless I've lost me blinking brain again and I'm all befuddled again an it's another day. But call it Tuesday. Discoveries, several. Three plates, broken. One cup, broken. One pan, no handle. Two coins amounting to two new pence and one old penny. A bag of bread, sodden. Umpteen pop bottles, plastic. One boot, one sock, one pair Y-fronts, extra large. One wing, kittiwake. One dog, black, dead. One large thigh bone, source unknown. Jewellery, none. Riches, none. Treasure, none. Mysteries, one.'

He chewed his pencil and stared down at us, lying in a row on his floor. I narrowed my eyes. I saw the bulge of his nose, the long hair hanging down, the outline of his ragged beard, the word SECURITY on his chest. He turned his face to the page again.

'Mysteries, one. Creatures, three, crawling on the Middens in the dead of night. One craft, timber. Three creatures carried here by water and the moon. Three creatures crawling from the depths of the Middens' mud. Three creatures, rescued by my Heaven.'

He lifted a piece of pie and started to chew it.

'There's visitors come, Grampa. Devils or angels or something in between? Who can say.'

He looked down at us, lying there on his floor. He wiped his sleeve across his mouth. He scribbled again.

'No doubt tomorrow will shed light.'

He leaned back in his creaking chair.

'Tuesday over,' he sighed. 'Wednesday still to come.'

He started to sing about the sea, about someone who had gone too far out and couldn't find the way home again. He sat there with his head lowered into the pool of candlelight. He glanced at us again.

'And if these is come for shenanigans,' he said. 'Then

mebbe there'll just be fettling to do.'

He smiled and sighed.

'Aye,' he said. 'A little bit of fettling.'

'It's Friday,' I whispered.

He stared.

'It's not Tuesday that's over. It's Friday,' I said.

He scratched his head. Black dust fell from it.

'Sorry,' I said.

He turned back the pages in his book.

'Friday,' he whispered. 'Friday over, Saturday to come. You're befuddled, Grampa.'

He stroked his beard.

'Ah, well. Ah, well.'

'Who are you?' I said.

'Who?'

'Where you from? Why are you here?'

His face twisted. He tilted his head and looked at me from the corner of his eye, as if he couldn't focus on me properly, as if I was a figment of his imagination.

'I remember many things,' he whispered. 'I remember I was all alone. I remember I did dig out Heaven Eyes one starry night from the mud of the Black Middens. Long long time ago. Long ago as she has been alive. I remember I am caretaker and always been the caretaker. But I do not remember many other things.'

He rubbed his eyes, focused on me, wrote again.

'You dug her out?' I said. 'What do you mean, you dug her out?'

'Grampa is the caretaker,' he said. 'Grampa dug out Heaven from the Middens one starry night. This is long long time back and much in memory does fade away. Heaven Eyes is called Heaven Eyes cos she does see through all the grief and trouble in the world to the Heaven that does lie beneath. There are days that come and nights that come and tides that turn. There is chocolates that are the sweetest chocolates of all.'

He fingered the peak of the helmet on his desk. His eyes cleared for a moment and he stabbed his finger towards me.

'No shenanigans! You hear? None of your shenanigans.'

'No,' I said.

He rolled his eyes and calmed again.

'Never mind. Tomorrow will shed light,' he murmured.

He sang again. I carefully moved Heaven's head from my arm and I stood up.

He watched me as I moved about the room. I touched the bones and the rusted tools. I stared down into boxes of shining pebbles. I felt the letters beneath my feet. There was a framed photograph on the wall: a young man in a uniform like Grampa's in brilliant sunshine by the river. I leaned close. Was this the same man, years and years ago? I turned and met his eye.

'You?' I said.

No answer. He looked right through me.

'Were you the caretaker, all those years ago?'

No answer. He turned his eyes away, went back to his writing.

There was a photograph of ships lined up on the quayside with great cranes above them, many men working on the quays in caps and boiler suits. There was a photograph of the greatest bridge as it was being built, the arms of the arch reaching towards each other across the water. There was a photograph of the printing works, lit by sunlight falling through the skylights, huge sheets of printed papers streaming out beneath the wings of eagles and angels.

January, Mouse and Heaven slept. Grampa murmured, sang and wrote. I went to his shoulder and looked down at his pages. At the head was printed: SECURITY REPORT, then DATE and NAME and POSITION. He had written *Tuesday*, crossed it out, replaced it with *Friday*, and written *Grampa* and *Caretaker*. The pages were crammed with tiny writing, with drawings of Heaven and her webbed fingers, with drawings of we three: black shapes on the Black Middens with the moon gleaming above. I saw our names recorded there: Erin, Janry and Mows.

'We came across the river,' I whispered.

'They crost the riva,' he whispered and wrote.

'We came from Whitegates in St Gabriel's.'

'They cum from Gaybrils.'

'We are damaged children, but we are happy.'

'They ar hapy hapy.'

'I once lived with my Mum. We had a little house above the river. It was our Paradise.'

I smiled as my story appeared beneath his hand, weaving its

way into the tale of Heaven Eyes, into the mysteries contained in his huge book.

'Write it,' I breathed. 'Everything is true. She was a little woman with red hair that grew like fire around her face and with brilliant green eyes . . . I had an Oxfam cot and pictures on the walls. We lived in that Paradise for ten short years . . .'

He went on writing: tiny words straggling over the wide page while black dust crumbled and fell from his fingers and hair.

'Mum,' I whispered. 'Look, Mum.'

I felt her hand on my shoulder, her breath on my face. She whispered my name. She whispered the black words of our story, reading it back to me as soon as I had told it.

'Everything is true,' I whispered.

'Evrythin is trew,' he wrote.

Then his hand stopped and turned his eyes to me. 'What you digging and searching for?'

'Nothing,' I said. 'Nothing.'

'Why you come here?'

'We were washed up on the Middens.'

'There is secrets,' he whispered.

His voice was harsh and threatening. He took out a key from his pocket. He opened the desk drawer and took out a carving knife. He held the blade before his face and he stared at me.

'Touch her and you is dead,' he hissed.

'What?'

'And you is dead.'

Heaven Eyes called me from the floor. She was still sleeping. I lay down beside her. Grampa watched and his eyes softened again.

'Erin,' she whispered in her sleep. 'Erin. My bestest friend.'

Grampa turned his eyes to the page again and was lost in his words again. Heaven whispered my name again. I looked across at Jan. He was asleep. He had heard nothing, seen nothing. I couldn't keep my eyes open. I took Heaven's hand in mine, held her as if for safety, then I fell deep into sleep.

Six

Her skin and hair glowed. Sunlight streamed through the skylights, through the outspread wings, over the huge printing machines. Metal letters glinted in the litter at our feet. Pigeons and sparrows fluttered over us. Little animals scratched in the shadows.

'Follow,' she kept saying. 'Follow, Erin, Janry and Mouse.

She led us from the printing works, into the lanes between the ruined buildings. We came to the edge of the Ouseburn and we paused there, at the head of steep steps that led down into the narrow gulley where the water flowed.

She reached out and clawed away dried mud from my throat with her webbed fingers.

'We will wash the Middens from us here,' she said.

She smiled.

'We will be all beautied again.'

On the opposite side of the Ousebum was a huge warehouse wall. To our left the water flowed into the wide glistening river.

'Keep little,' she whispered. 'Keep looking out, or the ghosts will eye us.'

'The ghosts?' I said.

'There is ghosts everywhere,' she said. 'We eye them past where the runny water runs. We eye them in little boats. We eye them running on machines. We eye them way way down there where the bridges is. We ear when they squeal and scream and fill the night with noise.'

She met January's eye.

'What matters, Janry Carr?' she said.

He glanced at me, glanced back at her. His hands were trembling.

'What matters, Janry Carr?' she said.

'We could just go,' he whispered to me. 'We could bloody go. We could even just go back to bloody Whitegates.'

'Where's your spirit of adventure?' I asked him.

'Hell's teeth, Erin,' he said.

'Do not be feared, Janry,' said Heaven Eyes.

'I'm not bloody frightened,' he hissed.

She touched him with her webbed hand. He stared in horror. He brushed the hand away.

'I is nice,' said Heaven. 'I will never never harm you.'

We watched each other, the three of us. Mouse slipped past us, and went down the steps to the Ouseburn.

'I'll wash first,' he said.

'Good Mouse,' said Heaven Eyes. 'Wash away all that filthy filth.'

She began to hum a slow sweet tune. January crouched,

stared at the broken ground, stabbed his penknife into the rubble.

I crouched beside him.

'You *are* scared,' I said. 'What is it? What you scared of?'

'I want to get out of this. I want to keep on, like we said we would. That's what the raft's for. That's what it was about.'

'We *can* go on, but not yet, Jan. Please, not yet.'

'You're hopeless,' he hissed. 'It was going to be just you and me and the raft and the river and look how it's ended up.'

I touched his shoulder. He tugged away.

'You're jealous,' I said. I laughed. 'That's what it is, isn't it? You want me and the journey all to yourself.'

'Yeah! If that's what you want to think, then think that.' I saw the tears shining in his eyes. 'But I tell you what. If you don't get out of the bloody spell I'll be off myself on the raft. Just me, travelling down to the sea. Just me, me.'

'Just me, me,' I mocked. I stood up again.

Mouse sat below at the edge of the Ouseburn, stripped to his underclothes with his feet dangling in the water. He threw handfuls of water over himself. He rubbed at the Middens mud with his hands.

Heaven smiled down at him. She took my hand. I glanced down at January. Then put my arm around Heaven Eyes.

'Where did you come from, Heaven Eyes?' I asked.

She shook her head.

'I memory little,' she said. 'There is nothing but a deep

deep dark. Grampa tells me this deep dark is the Middens. He tells me that he dug me out one moony night. That is all I memory, Erin Law, before Grampa and the printing works and the ghosts.'

'Nothing else?'

'Nothing else excepting sleep memories, and these I do not speak of for they must be wrong.'

'What are the sleep memories, Heaven Eyes?'

'Must never tell them. They does angry Grampa.'

She shifted closer to me.

'Grampa is old,' she said. 'Him does say that mebbe one day I must cross the river to the world of ghosts.'

She took a chocolate from a pocket and pressed it into my palm.

'For you,' she said. 'A chocolate that is the sweetest thing of all.'

Mouse climbed the steps again, dripping water. He smiled and smiled.

January shoved past us and went down to the water.

'You is beautied and happy, Mouse,' said Heaven Eyes.

Mouse laughed. He held Squeak in his gently closed fist.

Heaven touched the words tattooed on his forearm.

pLeAse LoOk aFter mE.

'What is these letters on you?' she asked.

'Please look after me,' said Mouse.

'Yes,' she said. 'I will truly please look after you.'

She pondered.

'But what is letters doing on your skin?'

'My Dad scratched them there,' he said. He lowered his eyes. 'He said one day I'd be on my own. He said I was weak and would always need to be protected. He got the idea from a book we used to read about a bear. He scratched them in with a knife and ink.'

She stroked his arm.

'You is not alone now, little Mouse,' she whispered.

'I know,' he said. He took Squeak out from his pocket. 'And I've always got this one, as well.'

He cupped his hands and Squeak tumbled through his fingers. He tipped Squeak into Heaven's hands and she laughed as the tiny creature scuttled and tumbled there.

'Lucky Mouse,' said Heaven Eyes. 'Lucky lucky Mouse.'

Squeak somersaulted and Heaven laughed. I saw how similar they were, Mouse and Heaven Eyes, how they were both like little children. Heaven passed Squeak back into Mouse's hands, then she held up her webbed fingers to the sunlight and said to me,

'What is a Dad, Erin?'

Then she ducked down.

'Ghosts!' she hissed.

She drew us back into a warehouse doorway.

'Janry,' she called. 'Keep little and still.'

Across the river, two cyclists pedalled on the cycle track towards the sea.

She smiled.

'All gone!' she whispered in delight.

She danced back on to the quay above the Ouseburn and her hair and her dress swirled around her.

'Happy,' she sang. 'Happy, happy, happy!'

Below her, January flung handfuls of black mud into the stream.

Seven

She giggled.

'Put in your hand, Erin Law,' she said.

She giggled again and spread her webbed hands across her mouth.

We had all been washed. There were just traces of the Middens in the creases in our skin, and its deep stains on our clothes. We were in one of the warehouses. There were piles of packing crates. Many of them were opened, like the one before us.

'Go on, go on,' she said.

I reached inside, angled my arm, stretched my hands, touched smooth cool cellophane-wrapped boxes.

'Feel?' she giggled. 'Feel, Erin?'

I lifted one of the boxes out, and I giggled too. It was a blue box of chocolates, Milk Tray.

'For you,' she said. 'For you and Janry and Mouse and Squeak. Go on, eat, eat!'

I peeled away the cellophane, opened it, passed around the whitening drying-out chocolates.

Heaven Eyes took an orange cream. She said it was her favourite. She licked her lips and sighed.

'Grampa says them will not last evermore,' she said. 'But there is lots in that crate an there is lots of crates.'

She showed us crates packed with Fray Bentos corned beef, with plastic packets of sultanas and currants. She showed us dozens of crates that still weren't opened.

I chewed a caramel.

'How old are you, Heaven Eyes?' I said.

She crinkled her eyebrows.

'No,' she said. 'I is not old. That is Grampa, Erin.'

'How many years are you, though?'

She gazed at me with her pale and shining eyes, so keen to please me, but all confused.

'How much time?' I said.

'Eat another,' she said. 'Go on and eat another. They lovely as lovely.'

January cursed. Mouse shoved Milk Tray into his mouth.

'How many days and nights?' I said.

'Day comes first, then night, then day again, round and round like dancing.'

'You don't understand,' I said.

She pondered.

'Life is wakes and sleeps,' she said. 'Is that what you is wanting?'

'How many wakes and sleeps have you been here?' I said.

She pondered. She giggled.

'You making my head flap like a pigeon wing, Erin.'

She peered into the chocolate box.

She pursed her lips.

'As many sleeps as there is orange creams,' she said.

January cursed.

'In this box?' he said.

'Oh, in the whole wide wide warehouse, Janry.'

'How many's that?'

She giggled and blushed. She turned her eyes away from January. She touched my arm with her hand and shuffled close to me.

'Three?' she whispered into my ear.

Eight

'On patrol, look.'

We were in a lane outside the food warehouse. Grampa was coming towards us. His jacket was buttoned up tight and he wore his peaked helmet. He swung his arms stiffly at his side. He carried an ancient black torch. He stopped at a little door and rattled its handle. He nodded, and scribbled something in a little notebook, then came on towards us again. We stepped back against the wall.

'Good morning, Grampa Caretaker,' said Heaven Eyes.

'Good morning, little Heaven. Anything to report?'

'Nothing, Grampa. Just ghosts running on machines way way out across the runny water.'

He nodded.

His brow furrowed as he stared at January, Mouse and me. Heaven Eyes stood on tiptoe, leaned on his shoulder, whispered to him.

'These is those that come last moony night. Memory, Grampa?'

He nodded again, and scribbled in his notebook again.

Then he raised his finger and peered into our eyes.

'I have you in this little book now,' he said. 'I will remember. No shenanigans, now.'

'No shenanigans,' I said.

He blinked, raised his helmet, scratched his head, gazed up into the brilliant blue sky. He slowly followed the flight of a seagull with his eyes. His face softened and he began to murmur a song. Then he blinked again and looked back at us.

'There is patrolling to be done,' he said.

Heaven Eyes reached up to him again and kissed his cheek.

'No shenanigans,' he said to me.

'No shenanigans,' I said.

He let Heaven kiss him again, then he walked on, peering into ancient doorways, rattling handles, scribbling in his book.

'He is that important, see,' said Heaven. 'He is caretaker.'

We wandered back towards the printing works. January kept watching me, shaking his head, cursing under his breath.

'Is there nobody else here?' he said to Heaven Eyes.

'What means you, Janry Carr?'

'Others. Other people.'

'There has been ghosts sometimes. We have hid from them, and if they have come too close then Grampa has fettled them.'

'Fettled them?'

'Yes, Janry. Fettled them.'

January looked at me.

'What did he do to them, Heaven Eyes?'

She shrugged.

'Things I does not know. Fettlings.'

'And there are no other caretakers.'

'Grampa is caretaker. Grampa.'

'Who pays him, then? Who does he report to? What does he do on his weekends off?'

Heaven clicked her tongue.

'Janry Carr, my head is flapping and rattling with you. Why not you be still a little bit?'

January shrugged. He took a chocolate from his pocket and chewed it.

Heaven Eyes took my hand.

'Grampa is busy as busy,' she said. 'Patrolling and caretaking in sunny days and digging and searching in moony nights.'

'Digging for what?' I said.

'Oh, lots of lovelies, Erin.'

'Will we see?'

'Mebbe under the shiny moon and shiny stars Erin will eye every little thing.'

I wanted to ask more, but I just shook my head and closed my eyes and grinned as my mind flapped and rattled and wouldn't be still.

We walked on. We entered the printing works and passed the great machines and entered the office.

'See?' said Heaven Eyes, showing us the things on the shelves, the bottles and rusty tools and shiny pebbles and bones. She stroked the dried-out wing of a seabird, its feathers all clotted with oil and mud. 'See? Lots of lovely lovelies.'

She linked me by the arm.

'And there is more lovelies, Erin. He says there is my treasure waiting to be dug one starry moony night. They will be dug up and chucked into his bucket.'

January snorted. He picked up the discoveries one by one from the shelves. He sighed in disgust. He stared up at the closed boxes by the ceiling. He turned over a few pages of Grampa's great book on the desk. He cursed. He sat against the wall, on his blanket, and scraped the mud from his trainers with his knife. Heaven Eyes watched him.

'Poor Janry Carr,' she whispered.

Mouse knelt by the table. He played with Squeak, letting him tumble through his fingers. Heaven smiled.

'Mouse and Squeak is happy but,' she whispered. 'Come. Come and sit.'

Nine

She led me towards the doorway. We sat down there against the open door. We leaned against each other. I touched the webs on her fingers, delicate things that gleamed with light. In front of us, sunbeams cascaded into the printing works. Dust danced there. Birds sang in the rafters. The sky beyond the broken skylights was brilliant blue, going on forever. A breeze blew across our faces.

'Who was your Mum, Heaven Eyes?' I asked.

Her eyes clouded. I smiled and tried again.

'Your Mum,' I said. 'Your Mummy. Your Mother.'

Her face crinkled.

'You and Janry Carr,' she said. 'Such funny mouthings from your mouths.'

'You don't understand?'

'Stand under what, Erin Law?'

I giggled.

'Just a sec,' I said.

I went to my blankets and got my rucksack. I took out my little cardboard treasure box and untied the ribbon.

'My Mum was a little woman with red hair and green eyes,' I said. 'She wore earrings like parrots and we lived together in a little house above the river. We were very happy and it was like Paradise.'

Heaven smiled and sighed.

'This is telling tales,' she said. 'Like Grampa telling tales about the black Black Middens. Lovely lovely. Tell, Erin. Tell the tales.'

She wriggled and eased closer against me.

I took out a photograph of Mum and me in our garden.

'This is us, see?' I said. 'There's me when I was little, and there's my Mum.'

She gazed down into the picture.

'You is like the ghosts,' she said.

I smiled. I heard Mum's giggling inside me.

'No,' I said. 'This is my Mum when she still was living.'

She chewed her lips and stared, like she was pondering some great mystery. I showed her the parrot earring.

'What's mums, Erin?' she said.

'Mums are what we come from. There are Dads as well.'

Her face crinkled.

I dug into the treasure box again. She giggled and squirmed.

'This is your treasures, Erin, isn't it?'

'Yes.'

'Lovely lovely. My treasures is waiting in the Middens says Grampa. He will dig them out afore he is still as still.'

'Still as still?'

'Still as still. Not mind, Erin. Show, show.'

I took out the blurry photograph from the hospital, the scan that showed me growing inside her. You could see my head, my arms waving, my legs kicking.

'This is me,' I said. 'This is me when I was inside my Mum. This is me months before I was born.'

She giggled. She looked at me and at the photograph.

'You's fibbing?' she said.

'No. This is me inside my Mum.'

She stared again.

'Is dark as dark in there. Is hard to eye proper.'

'Yes,' I whispered. 'Dark as dark.'

'You memory it?'

'No, I don't remember it.'

'No nor me.'

'Nor you?'

'I was in the black Black Middens where all is black as black. Grampa dug me out into the sunny days and moony nights.'

'You must have had a Mum,' I whispered.

She pondered.

'So the black Black Middens was the Mum.' She laughed, delighted, and she squeezed me tight. 'The Mum of Erin Law was dark as dark. The Mum of Heaven Eyes was black as black.'

We sat there in silence for a time.

'How did you get into the Black Middens?' I said. She sighed.

'This is mystery, Erin Law. Grampa says that mebbe once I was a fishy thing or a froggy thing swimming in the water.'

She looked at the photograph of me inside my Mum again.

She beamed.

'And eye this proper,' she said. 'Eye them little hands and little feet. Eye little Erin flapping like in water.'

'Yes,' I said.

'Erin Law, you was also once a fishy thing or a froggy thing.'

I laughed.

'Yes,' I said.

'Erin is like Heaven Eyes and Heaven Eyes is like Erin.'

'Yes,' I said.

We grinned at each other.

'Fishy,' I said.

'And froggy,' she said.

We laughed and laughed. How would we ever make proper sense to each other? I put my arms around her and squeezed her tight and she wriggled, just like a little sister would.

'You!' I said.

'Me?'

'Yes, you! You! What am I going to do with you?'

'Do nothing, Erin Law. Just stay and be my friend. And just be careful.'

'Careful?'

'Yes, my sister. For there is holes here. There is places to tumble out the world and not get found again.'

I laughed again and dug into the treasure box. I took out the bottle of perfume. I tipped it on to my finger. I touched the perfume on to my neck and on to Heaven's neck. I felt Mum beside us. She held both of us in her arms.

'Lovely,' whispered Heaven.

'Lovely,' I whispered.

'Lovely,' whispered Mum.

Ten

January kicked my feet.

'Outside,' he hissed.

I rubbed my eyes.

'Outside, Erin.'

Heaven dozed against me, holding my arm with her webbed hand.

January glared at me.

'Come on,' he said.

I moved Heaven's hand away, stood up, went through the door with him into the printing works. He led me between the machines, stood beneath a huge cast-iron eagle.

'We've got to go,' he said.

I said nothing.

'We've got to bloody go.'

'Soon,' I said.

We walked on. Through a massive doorway we saw the river running, the opposite bank. Grampa strode past with his arms dead stiff and the torch in his hands.

'We've got to get away from them,' he said.

'Oh, January,' I said.

'He's mad and she's a freak. Have you seen her bloody hands?'

'Something awful's happened to her. I just know it, Jan.'

'Something awful'll happen to us if we stay. There's a bloody big axe under his desk. Did you know that?'

'No.'

'Well, then.'

'It's to protect her.'

'Aye, but what if he decides to protect her from us, eh?'

'He wouldn't harm us.'

'Ha!'

He kicked and metal letters scattered and chinked across the floor.

'What about the raft?' he said. 'What about the river? What about getting miles and miles away?'

'But this is miles and miles away. Does it not feel like that?'

'Feels like a nightmare, Erin. Worse than that. Feels like a mad place, an evil place.'

'Evil!'

He kicked again and cursed. Grampa passed by the door again, dead stiff, the peak of his helmet glinting in the sunlight.

'Look at him!' he hissed.

'Ha!' I laughed.

'It's like you're under a spell.'

'Ha!'

I pushed a chocolate into my mouth, pushed another into

his hand. He threw it at the eagle. He kicked the letters, then he calmed himself.

'It feels like death, Erin. That's what it feels like. It feels like if we don't leave soon, we'll never get away.'

We faced each other, unblinking.

'Ha!' I said again, more quietly.

Then I lowered my eyes.

'We will get away,' I whispered. 'We will, Jan.'

We ran our feet through the letters on the floor.

'Look,' he said. 'At least let's check the raft's all right, so we can make a quick getaway.'

We walked towards the river. We heard Grampa's footsteps nearby. We spotted him watching from a doorway in an alley. I sucked a butterscotch. A pair of herring gulls were squabbling on the quay, lungeing at each other with their long sharp beaks. They hopped away as we approached. They continued to fight, beaks clacking and scratching, voices screeching. We came to the end of the alleyways.

I giggled.

'Look out for ghosts,' I said.

'Ghosts! Bloody ghosts!'

We went to the edge, looked down. The Middens were covered with running water. The raft floated there, tugging at its rope. January sighed with relief.

'See?' I said.

'Aye. But somebody's going to see it and they're going to come and get us and it's back to Maureen and the rest.'

'We could pull it out,' I said.

'We've got to get away.'

He glared at the raft.

'I'll go without you,' he said.

He looked sideways at me.

'I will,' he said.

I saw the anger in his eyes. But I saw the fear as well. He needed me to tell him not to go. He needed me to tell him I'd leave Heaven Eyes and Grampa and come with him. Heaven's words kept running through my head: You is my sister . . . You is my bestest friend . . . I couldn't leave her alone in the printing works with Grampa. Part of me already loved her as a sister. I didn't know how to say this to Jan.

'It was going to be our adventure,' he said. 'Just you and me and the raft and the river. Then you let stupid Mouse come. Then you let two stupid freaks put you under a spell!'

'Go on, then,' I said. 'Go off on your own.'

Then I reached for his hand, but before I could touch him we heard footsteps behind us. The herring gulls swooped up into the sky. Grampa was stamping through an alley towards us. He had a carving knife in his hands. He held it high above his head. Its blade glittered in the sun. His face was red as blood beneath its creases of black. His eyes glared, filled with death.

January stepped in front of me. He gripped his own glittering knife in his raised fist.

'Come on, then!' he yelled. 'Come on, old man!'

Heaven Eyes came running through the alleyways.

'No!' she yelled. 'These is my friends, Grampa!'

She caught his shoulder. She wrapped her arms around him.

'Grampa! These is my friends that come in the moony night!'

He stood there panting. His eyes cleared. The knife dangled from his hands. Heaven Eyes clung on to him and whispered desperately to him.

Jan kept his knife raised high. His body was tense, poised. His breath came in short deep gasps.

'Shame she come,' he hissed. 'Could have finished it, here and now.'

Heaven Eyes turned Grampa away. She started to lead him back through the alley. She kept turning. Her eyes pleaded with us not to go away.

'Knife in the heart,' said Jan. 'Or in the throat, or in the guts. Easy.'

'You weren't scared?'

'He's an old man. He's cracked. Wouldn't have a chance.'

I was trembling. I wanted to run to Heaven Eyes and comfort her.

'We've seen it, though,' said Jan.

'What?'

He grabbed me by the shoulders and glared at me. He spat out the words one by one.

'He's a bloody killer, Erin. This place is mad and evil. We have to go away.'

He dragged my face towards him. He narrowed his eyes.

'Why d'you want to stay when you know we could all die here?'

I chewed my lips and felt tears trickling on my cheeks.

'Don't leave me,' I wanted to say. 'Please don't leave me, Jan.'

But I said nothing.

He pushed me away, jumped over the ancient quay, scrambled down the ancient ladder and leapt across the water on to the raft. He stood over the red curse while the river tugged at the tightly fastened rope. I watched him, waited for him to sail away all alone and leave me all alone. But he didn't untie it. He just stood there swaying with the movements of the water, his head filled with fury and dreams of freedom, and disappointment with me, his best friend.

Eleven

I tried to shout at him. 'Jan! January!' But my voice was a hopeless whimper, and he didn't turn. He'd given up on me. I left him and turned back to the dark alleyways, the dilapidated quays, the broken buildings, the ruins of the past, the place he said was mad, was evil, the place he said was death. I kicked my way through ancient litter and fallen rubble. The walls and ceilings creaked and groaned. Dust seethed all around me. Shadows shifted. Dark birds flapped above. Dangling doors led into pitch-black rooms and offices. The ground was cracked and potholed. In places it had simply fallen away, and yawning gaps showed cavernous cellars below. I imagined ghosts all around me, watching me, the ghosts of those who had worked here and filled the place with noise and light and life. I felt their fingers touching me as I walked, heard their hollow breathing, their whispering, their sad laughter. I imagined beasts staring out at me from the deepest darkest places. I saw their eyes glittering, saw their raised claws glinting. They were creatures that had grown in darkness and desolation, mutant life forms, half-dead and half-alive. They grabbed at me as I passed by, they hissed my name, they tried to drag me to them, tried to make me theirs. I kept walking, walking, walking. I walked through my own mind, through my memories and hopes and dreams. I kicked the litter, breathed the dust. I remembered walking down to the raft again for the first time with January when we felt so light and free. We spun out on to the river and hugged each other. Freedom. Freedom. A new beginning. So how had we come so quickly to this dark dilapidated dangerous place? How had we been so quickly thrown apart? I saw him drifting alone down river on the raft, drifting into the endless empty sea. I saw him raising his arms in joy. Freedom! he yelled. Freedom! I pushed through a dangling door. Darkness. I shuddered and groaned. I held my hands out in front of me and went deeper, deeper. I edged my way past the sad ghosts, came to an opening in the floor. I went down, down. Ancient crumbling steps. The stench of damp and rot and doom. I went down into the deepest darkness until there was nowhere left to go, just the furthest corner of the furthest cellar. I lay down in the slime.

'Mum,' I whispered.

No answer.

I found her hand resting in mine. Her hand grew colder, colder. I held it as she closed her eyes for the last time. I held it as she disappeared, as she left me all alone. It grew colder, colder.

'Why did you die?' I said to her. 'Why? Why?'

No answer.

'Mum,' I whispered. 'Mum. Please, Mum!'

No answer. Just her hand in mine. Just her cold, still, dead hand in mine.

I lay down at her side in silence. The cold and stillness entered my bones. I lay there in the slime as the mutants gathered around me. The scratch of their claws replaced my mum's caressing touch. Their vicious hiss replaced her voice. I moved beyond words, beyond laughter, beyond tears. No hope. No joy. No life. Death grew all around and drew me in.

Twelve

'Erin Law! Erin Law!'

Her voice echoed through the alleyways and the buildings and found its way through the dangling door, past the ghosts and mutants, into my deep darkness.

'Erin Law! Erin Law!'

It found its way into my head and called me back from silence, emptiness, deadness.

'Erin Law! Erin Law!'

I rubbed my face and felt the thick slime on my skin, in my hair. I retched and spat. I sat up and tried to call her but I only gasped and croaked.

'Erin Law! Erin Law!'

I stood up and tottered through the darkness with my hands held out in front of me, but I was sore and stiff and I stumbled and fell into the stony litter.

'Heaven!' I tried to shout. 'Heaven!'

I crawled, but couldn't tell if I was crawling to the light or deeper into the dark.

'Heaven!' I called. 'Heaven Eyes!'

I wiped my face and tasted the blood that trickled from my hands.

'Heaven Eyes!'

'Erin Law!'

Her voice was closer, clearer. I strained to hear her footsteps through whatever walls and floors surrounded me.

'Where is you, Erin Law'

I wiped tears from my eyes.

'I don't know,' I whispered.

'I'm here!' I called. 'Here I am!'

'Erin Law! Erin Law! Erin Law!'

I stumbled and crawled and tried to find the ancient stairway, tried to climb out of the stench of damp and doom. But crawled in useless circles, crawled to places where there were cracks and chasms in the floor, where there were more stairways heading down, openings to even deeper cellars. I felt the mutants' fingers, urging me down. I heard their hiss. 'Yes. Yesss. Further down. Further down.' I struggled with them. I tried to focus on Heaven Eye's voice, but it was tiny, distant, something from another world. I told myself I was lost, never to be found, that I had gone too deep into impenetrable dark, that no one could ever find me and help me out. 'Further down,' the voices hissed. 'Yes. Further down.' I stopped crawling. I held my Mum's hand again for the final time as she closed her eyes for the final time.

'Erin Law! Erin Law!'

The voice circled and searched and faded and grew and faded again and would not give up.

'Erin Law! Where is you, Erin Law?'

'I don't know,' I wept.

I sobbed. I held my Mum's dead hand.

'I don't know!' I called.

I lay down in the slime again. I felt the coldness entering my bones again.

'Here!' I called.

I closed my eyes. The voice circled and searched and circled and searched. I went back deep into my dark.

'Erin Law!'

It was closer.

'I eye you, Erin Law.'

I grunted.

'Keep still. Keep still as still.'

'What?'

'I eye you. Keep still and Heaven Eyes will come to you.'

I stared into the dark, saw nothing. Impossible to see anything in such deep deep dark. Heard the footsteps in the litter coming nearer, heard her breath as she came nearer, heard the rustle of her clothes as she came nearer. But saw nothing. Then the touch of her fingers on my face.

'Oh my sister Erin Law! What is you doing in this deep deep dark?'

Thirteen

'I did tell you,' she said. 'I did tell you there is holes in the ground where the darkness and the dangers is. You must watch out for them, my sister.'

She wiped the slime from my face with her gentle fingers.

'There is places to tumble out the world and not be found again,' she said. 'You must watch out for them.'

We stood beyond the dangling door in the rubble and litter below a broken roof. She stroked my face. My eyes stung, adjusting to the light. My head reeled.

'What is this place?' I said.

No answer.

'What is it? Is it evil? Is it mad?'

'What is you mouthing, Erin Law?'

'What are you?' I whispered.

'I is Heaven Eyes, my sister.'

'What is Grampa?'

'He is my Grampa, my sister.'

'What is this place?'

'Is the place of Heaven Eyes and Grampa, my sister.'

Birds sang and flapped through ruined rafters high above. Things sighed and slithered through the cellars below.

'Is it life?' I said. 'Or is it death?'

She blinked, confused. She touched my face again.

'What is you been thinking of deep down there, my sister?'

She pushed a chocolate into my hand. I put it into my mouth and chewed.

'Sweet,' I told her.

'Sweetest thing of all,' she grinned. 'Take more. Take more.'

'What can I ask that you can answer?'

She shrugged and smiled.

'Ask nothing. Just chew the chocolate that is the sweetest thing of all.'

'Why does Grampa want to kill us?'

'Grampa is a good Grampa. He will never never harm you.'

I shook my head and laughed softly.

'So what about the knife, Heaven Eyes?'

'He did unmemory you.'

'Unmemory?'

'He did think you was ghosts or devils come to do shenanigans.'

'He wanted to kill us, Heaven.'

'Mebbe. So you must stay close with Heaven Eyes. You must never never be like ghosts. You must say Good Day, Grampa Caretaker. You must tell him that Heaven is loveliest of lovelies.'

'What else?' I said.

'Nothing else. And Grampa will be kind.'

I laughed again.

'Kind!'

'Come see,' she said.

I let her lead me by the hand towards the printing works. I kept turning towards the water, wanting to see Jan, but saw nothing. Then outside the office we saw him, lounging against a printing machine. I gasped with relief and spoke his name. He watched us coldly. I said his name again and he just shrugged. I ached to reach out to him. I ached for him to speak to me but he said nothing. I took a deep breath and let Heaven lead me into the office. The day was ending and the candles were burning. Grampa was scribbling in his great book. He munched at a slab of Fray Bentos corned beef. His helmet was on the desk beside him.

'See?' Heaven said. 'Grampa is gentle now. He does unmemory many many things. He does write down many things an that is his memorying.'

I looked at the great book. I watched his hand writing furiously. I imagined the thousands upon thousands of words that he must have written in this room by candlelight.

'He must have written much about you?' I said.

'Many many much, Erin. Many many many much while Heaven Eyes eats chocolates and sleeps and has funny thoughts and funny sleep memories.'

'Have you read his books, Heaven?'

Her face crinkled.

'Have you read the things he has written?'

'He has writ that Heaven Eyes is loveliest of lovelies, Erin Law.'

'But what else?'

'Else nothing.'

January cursed from the doorway. He came towards us.

'She can't bloody read,' he said. He glared at her. 'So where's all his books, then?'

She chewed her lips.

'Oh, Janry Carr, this is one thing that does angry him.'

'What does?'

'There is Grampa's secrets, Janry Carr. No looking. No touching.'

January gazed about the room.

'Where are the secrets, Heaven Eyes?'

I felt her hand tremble against my arm.

'Tell Janry Carr he must stopping now,' she whispered.

January laughed.

'Tell Janry Carr he must not be like them ghosts looking and searching.'

'You hear?' I said to January.

He hissed. He glared at me.

Grampa turned his eyes towards us. They glittered in the candlelight. They softened as they fell upon Heaven. She smiled at him.

'I does love you, Grampa,' she whispered.

'Love,' he murmured and wrote. 'Love, love, love. Heaven Eyes and Grampa. Love, love, love.'

'There,' said Heaven. 'You does eye what gentleness he has? You does eye how he is kind?'

'Yes,' I said.

'Yes. He will do no harm.'

January cursed under his breath.

Mouse watched us from the shadows in a corner. Squeak tumbled through his fingers.

Soon, Grampa rose from the table. He took his jacket off.

'Turn round,' said Heaven Eyes.

We turned our eyes away. We heard Grampa undressing. When we looked back again, he wore nothing but a pair of black knee-length shorts. His skin was blue-grey, with tracks of black sediment in the creases. He had a tattoo of an anchor on his hairy chest. His legs were skinny, he had a little pot belly, but there were great muscles on his arms and shoulders. He went to the door and pulled on a pair of huge boots. He bent down and kissed Heaven Eyes and his hair and beard fell over her pale shining face. He picked up a spade and a bucket and stepped out into the darkening night.

'He is off treasuring,' said Heaven and her eyes widened in excitement. 'And mebbe tonight's the moony night when Heaven's treasure is chucked into the bucket.'

'Can we go with him?' I asked.

She smiled.

'Oh, Erin,' she said. 'Most definite you can. Come on, Janry Carr. Come, on, Mouse and Squeak. Let's eye Grampa digging in the moony starry night.'

Fourteen

The sky glittered above the warehouses. We stumbled in potholes and grazed our knuckles on stone. Heaven glided before us, pale hair waving gently as she walked. Beyond her, the black shape of Grampa lurched towards the river. Closer to the river we saw the sky burning above the city. Hundreds of tiny lights marked the bridge's arch. Distant steeples and blocks of flats were silhouetted against the sky. The river glowed like polished metal beneath the moon. There was far-off squealing from Norton Quays. Grampa stooped down, then turned and lowered himself on to the ancient ladder. His eyes glittered as he stared back at us.

'Good evening, Grampa Caretaker!' called Heaven. 'This is me with my friends, Erin, Janry and Mouse. We is patrolling and watching for ghosts.'

He raised his hand, then descended.

We squatted above and watched. He went to the raft and inspected it. He traced his fingers over January's curse. Then he walked on and we heard his feet slopping and slithering in the mud. He started to dig. There were great sucks and slaps as he lifted the Middens, spadeful by spadeful. Water drained and splashed. He laid a heap of mud beside him, then crouched beside it and sifted through it with his fingers. He discovered many things. He held them up to the moon. He scraped away the mud on them. He threw some of them out into the river. He put others into his bucket. Then he lay down at the hole he had dug and reached deep down into it. He reached arm-deep into the Middens and searched and searched. New discoveries were thrown out into the river or dropped into the bucket. Then he shoved the heap back into the hole. He lifted the bucket, went to another part of the Middens, and began again. We lay down on the broken ground, faces dangling over the edge. A smell of oil and rot and fish rose from the Black Middens below. Sometimes a sudden stench passed over us and we gagged and held our breath until it had drifted away. Grampa slithered and dug and the moon shone down on him and he was like some ancient creature struggling there, like something made of the Middens mud himself.

Mouse was wide-eyed and staring. He came close to me.

'This is like me,' he said. 'Like me, digging in the dirt for treasures.'

I laughed.

'Yes,' I said. 'He's just like you.'

'There'll be all sorts in there,' he said, 'washed down by the river. There'll be things from centuries back.'

He looked at Heaven Eyes.

'Could I go and help him?' he said.

'Oh, Mouse,' she said. 'That will be so nice for Grampa to have his little helper. Yes, Mouse, go and help. Grampa!' she called. 'My friend Mouse is coming down to help in digging for the treasure.'

Grampa turned, his eyes glittered, he waved.

Mouse held Squeak up to his face.

'Mouse is off to help Grampa find secrets,' he said. 'Just like you help me.'

He passed Squeak from his hands into mine.

'Look after him,' he said.

Squeak's tiny sharp claws scrabbled on my palm. He peered out from my gently closed fist as Mouse left us.

'Eek,' he squeaked. 'Eek. Eek.'

Mouse descended the ladder. He crouched on the Middens and started digging with his bare hands.

'What's the treasure he's searching for?' I said to Heaven Eyes.

'Treasure for Heaven Eyes.'

'What is it, though?'

'He does say that there is many treasure and secrets in these Middens. They has been carried there from way way back. He does say that one night he will find them and he will chuck them in his bucket.'

We watched again.

Jan sat up and stared towards the sea.

The sucking and slapping went on below.

'Has he found any of the treasure yet?' I said.

'Little bits. He does say that he will discover more afore he is still as still.'

'Still as still?'

'Still as still. And he does say that the bestest of all treasures is already dug, and that treasure is his Heaven Eyes that he did dig out one moony starry night.'

January sneered.

'And he chucked you in the bucket, eh?'

'Oh, Janry Carr. I's too big for buckets. Does you not eye that?'

January started prowling the quay behind us.

I lay close to Heaven. I touched the webs on her fingers. She gazed at me with her huge pale shining eyes.

'And are there other Heaven Eyes in the Middens?' I asked her.

She blinked and pondered.

'This is just mystery, Erin. But he does say that one day he might dig out Heaven's brothers an Heaven's sisters. He does say that they will care for Heaven Eyes when Grampa is still as still.'

I put my arm around her.

'Heaven,' I whispered. 'Do you really think you have brothers and sisters somewhere?'

'In these black Black Middens, yes.'

'In other places, though. In the past.'

'There is funny thoughts and sleep memories. In these there is mebbe sisters and brothers and many many strange things. But these we must not talk of, for they does angry Grampa.'

'But could we whisper of them some time?'

She reached up and touched my cheek.

'Mebbe,' she whispered. 'Mebbe, mine sister.'

And we lay together watching Grampa and Mouse, while Squeak tumbled through my fingers, and did not notice that January had left us there.

Fifteen

'Where is Janry Carr?' said Heaven.

Below us, Grampa was digging his third hole. Mouse lay flat on the Middens with both arms deep into the mud. Heaven Eyes sat up and looked back towards the buildings.

'Where is Janry Carr?'

'Dunno,' I said.

'Oh, Erin,' she said.

'He'll be OK,' I said. I laughed. 'He's a big boy, you know.'

'But him has shenanigans on his mind, Erin.'

'Should I go and find him?'

She chewed her lips.

'Both us go, Erin. And we must look very first in Grampa's office.'

We slipped away from the quay. I put Squeak into my pocket. We hurried through the alleyways and entered the printing works. Candlelight glinted through the boarded-up window of the office. Heaven hurried to the door and listened. Her eyes were filled with fear when she looked at me.

'Janry Carr is in there,' she whispered. 'Unless it is a ghost.'

I heard him, moving about inside.

'You go,' she said. 'You go tell Janry Carr to stop.'

I turned the handle.

January was climbing on the shelves. He was halfway up the wall, reaching higher. He grinned when he saw me.

'Down!' called Heaven Eyes. 'Down, down!'

She pushed me forward.

'Tell,' she said. 'Tell Janry Carr down, down.'

'Get down,' I said.

He held out a pair of rusty scissors and the bleached skeleton of a little fish.

'Treasure!' he said.

Heaven Eyes was sobbing.

'Get down,' I said again.

'Get down!' said Heaven Eyes. 'You will angry Grampa. He will do his fettling on you.'

Jan jumped back from the shelves and landed beside me.

'But up there,' he said, pointing up to the highest shelves where dusty boxes rested. 'Mebbe there'll be something up there.'

'No, Janry Carr,' said Heaven Eyes. 'You must never go up there. You must never look inside them boxes.'

He just laughed.

'And look,' he said, crouching beside the desk. He showed me the locked drawer. 'What about in there, eh?'

He took his penknife from his pocket. He unfolded a thin blade and pushed it into the lock.

'Tell him stop!' sobbed Heaven. 'Just tell him stop.'

I grabbed his hand. He laughed.

'OK,' he said.

Heaven leaned on me and wept into her webbed hands. January winked.

'But when they're both out, eh?' he whispered.

I glared back at him, but I knew that I wanted to open the boxes and the drawer just as much as he did.

We sat down against the wall. I fed Heaven orange creams. I whispered that January would never never do those things again. I took Squeak from my pocket. I passed him to her. She watched as he tumbled through her fingers. She calmed down.

'You's so nice, Erin,' she whispered. She nuzzled against me. 'And Janry Carr's so nasty sometime.'

Soon we heard footsteps crossing the printing floor. Grampa and Mouse came in, Grampa in his shorts, Mouse in his underclothes. They were soaked, water was running from them. Mouse's eyed blazed with joy.

'Magic!' he said. 'Magic!'

He knelt on the floor, opened his hands, spilled out a little heap of discoveries. There were blue pebbles, the skull of a tiny animal, a coin, a red cup handle, a green plastic bowl.

'See?' he said. 'There must be so much there in that mud just waiting to be found.'

Grampa carried his bucket to the desk. He laid his discoveries on the table. He put his clothes back on.

'We dug,' said Mouse. 'We dug and dug. I felt like I could

go on digging to the middle of the world. Then the river started coming back again. We got washed in the Ouseburn.' He stared up at Grampa. 'The things he must have found!' he whispered.

Heaven Eyes stood with her arm around Grampa. She watched him with pride.

'Tuesday,' said Grampa as he wrote. 'Or some other day. Discoveries, several. Pie tins, one, rusted. One penny. Umpteen pop bottles, plastic. One hammer, minus handle. Two fish hooks, large and small. Objects slung into the river, many. Jewellery, none. Riches, none. Treasure, none. Helpers, one . . .'

'That's Mouse,' said Heaven.

She beamed at us.

'That's my friend, Mouse, Grampa. That's who your little helper is.'

'Name Mouse,' muttered Grampa as he wrote.

He turned his head and looked at Mouse as if amazed to see him there.

He wrote again.

'One helper come out of the night, come out of the black Black Middens to help in the digging and the search for Heaven's treasure.'

'He will help you every night,' said Heaven.

Grampa pondered, then he wrote again.

'NB. Memory this, Grampa. This helper must have bucket, one, boots, two.'

Heaven Eyes gasped.

'Bucket and boots, Mouse! Grampa must be much much happy with you helping.'

Sixteen

It was in the middle of that night that we were all woken by Grampa.

'Ghosts!' he called. 'Ghosts! Ghosts!'

We sat up from our beds on the floor.

Grampa was standing by the shelves. He held a broken bird's wing in his hand. There was a broken bottle on the floor at his feet.

Heaven rushed to him.

'There has been ghosts in here, little Heaven,' he said.

He pointed to the shoeprint in the black dust on the shelves. I trembled. It was the unmistakable mark of Jan's running-away trainers. Grampa stared up at the closed boxes by the ceiling. He tried to climb the shelves but he was unsteady and he tumbled down again.

His face was red and strained.

'Nobody's been,' I whispered.

He stared, as if he stared right through me.

'Ghosts!' he whispered.

Heaven trembled. She gripped his arm with her webbed

fingers.

January rose and came to us.

'Nobody's been,' he said.

Grampa looked down at Mouse.

'You is my Little Helper?' he said.

'Yes,' said Heaven. 'Yes, he is your Little Helper.'

Tears were trickling down her cheeks.

'Climb,' said Grampa. 'Go up where them boxes are. Check them isn't opened, Little Helper.'

Mouse rubbed the sleep from his eyes and started to climb. I stood beneath him, ready to catch him if he fell. He reached the top shelf.

'Is them boxes tight?' said Grampa.

Mouse stretched, shaking the lids of the boxes one by one.

'Yes,' he said.

'Is them ropes and belts still fastened tight?'

'Yes.'

Grampa sighed.

'Come on down, then,' he whispered.

His eyes were red-rimmed. He stared at the footprint. He scratched his beard and the black dust fell from it. He looked old, old. He held Heaven against him.

'See?' she whispered.

He pointed to the footprint. She reached out and swept it away with her fingers.

'Is nothing,' she whispered, and her voice was shaking.

He licked his lips, lost in the mystery.

'Is nothing,' Heaven said again. 'You is having sleep

thoughts and imaginings, Grampa.'

'There is been no ghosts?' he said.

'There is been no ghosts, Grampa.'

She led him back to his desk. He sat there gazing into nothingness while she stroked his head. Then he lifted his pencil and started scribbling again.

Heaven Eyes lay down beside me and wept.

I stroked her hair.

'It'll be all right,' I said.

'No, Erin. Never no.'

She twisted and turned for hours, unable to sleep.

'That Janry Carr!' she hissed. 'That Janry Carr! He has got me telling fibs and lies and wrongnesses. Oh, Erin. Oh, my sister Erin Law.'

Seventeen

The boots were dried-out and twisted. Massive toecaps stuck out way beyond his toes. The tops came almost to his knees. Grampa lashed them around Mouse's calves with string. The shorts were navy blue and hung on Mouse's body like a frock. The shovel had a thick bleached timber handle and a rusted blade. Mouse stood before us blinking. His body was pale, skinny and bony. His cheeks burned with embarrassment and pride. Squeak crouched at his feet, looked up at him and squeaked.

Heaven clapped her hands with joy.

'Oh Mouse! Oh little lovely Mouse! How lovely you does look!'

She gazed into my eyes.

'Tell him, Erin! Tell him how lovely him does look!'

I straightened my face.

'Yes,' I said. 'You look lovely, Mouse.'

Grampa stood at a distance and pondered.

'You does look fine, little helper,' he said. 'Your bucket is at the door next to mine. Tonight we will go out digging and treasuring.'

'OK, Grampa,' said Mouse.

He raised his hand to his brow, like a salute.

Heaven giggled.

'Did you hear? Did you hear? "OK, Grampa." Just like a proper helper. Oh, Mouse. We is that proud of you! Now we will get that treasure even faster!'

She popped a chocolate cream into her mouth and skipped around the room. Grampa put his helmet on. He fastened his jacket tight. Heaven calmed herself.

'Time for patrolling, Grampa,' she said.

'Time for patrolling.'

He looked up at the shelves, at the boxes by the ceiling. He leaned close to the shelf where the footprint had been. He pondered.

He took a key from his pocket and opened the drawer in his desk. He took out the carving knife.

'We must be careful, Heaven Eyes,' he said.

'Yes, Grampa. We must be careful as careful.'

She made a face at January as Grampa wrapped the knife in a cloth and angled it down into his jacket pocket.

Grampa locked the drawer again. He kissed Heaven Eyes. He saluted Mouse. He looked through January and me as if we weren't there. Then he stepped out into the printing works.

'Get those stupid things off, Mouse,' said January.

Mouse blinked and blushed. He leaned the shovel against the wall and lifted his clothes from the bed.

Heaven shook her head sadly.

'Let's go wandering and talking about mums and dads and treasures, Erin,' she whispered.

'OK,' I said.

I glared at January. I pointed at him.

'Don't do it again,' I said.

He winked. He spoke like Heaven Eyes.

'As if I would, Erin, my bestest bestest friend.'

He sighed.

'Anyway, I'm starving.'

'There is chocolates an corned beef,' said Heaven Eyes.

'Chocolates and corned beef!'

He went to the door.

'I'll see what else there is, eh?'

'Be careful,' I said.

'Careful!'

'Remember the knife.'

He grinned and patted his pocket, where his own knife rested. He strolled out into the printing works. Heaven shook her head sadly. She took my hand.

'That Janry Carr,' she whispered.

Then her face brightened again.

'Come on, Erin. Come and tell me all those funny tales about mums and dads.'

We sat together in the doorway again and leaned against each other. We talked of these great mysteries while Grampa patrolled and Jan plundered and Mouse played and whispered to little Squeak.

Jan returned, ages later, with a box in his arms. He dropped it on to the ground in front of us. It was filled with food and drink: tins of beans and peas and fruit; packets of biscuits; tomato ketchup; boxes of dried milk; cereals; cans of Coke; jars of coffee; packets of tea.

'It's like a bloody treasure house out there!' he laughed.

Heaven stared wide-eyed with her hands against her face.

Jan shoved a bar of fruit-and-nut chocolate into my hand. He ripped open a packet of Hob Nobs and held it towards Heaven.

'Go on,' he said. 'Take one.'

'These things is to last for long long long, Janry Carr,' she said.

'And they will ! You could feed an army with what's out there.'

'And there is great joy in knowing that there is boxes waiting forever to be opened.'

'Great joy! Go on, take one. Take one.'

She chewed her lips.

'And what will Grampa say?'

'Grampa!'

He shoved a biscuit into his mouth and chewed. He sighed with pleasure. She reached out and touched the packet.

'Grampa will know nothing,' whispered Jan. 'Take one. Go on, be a devil.'

She leaned on me as she reached out and took one, as she lifted it to her mouth and began to nibble.

'Nice?' I said.

'Mmm. Nice as nice.'

She looked down into the box.

'We must hide these things,' she said. 'They will angry Grampa.'

'Where could we hide them?' said Jan.

She pointed to one of the biggest printing machines.

'Mebbe in the darkness under there,' she said. 'He will not eye them.'

Jan scuttled across the floor with the box. He crouched and shoved it into the darkness. He grinned back at us.

'Good idea, Heaven Eyes,' he said.

Heaven chewed her lips. She leaned on me.

'I is getting bad,' she said.

'No, you're not,' I said.

Jan winked at her.

She looked sideways at me, and blushed.

Eighteen

Night. The moon shone down. Music blared from distant Norton Quays. We lay together on the broken ground, gazing down to the Black Middens. January was somewhere in the shadows behind us. Mouse and Grampa splashed together across the mud. Mouse slithered and stumbled in his new boots. He dragged his heavy bucket and shovel behind him.

'You must be that proud,' said Heaven Eyes. 'Your friend Mouse as Grampa's Little Helper.'

'Yes, Heaven Eyes.'

I slipped her a Hob Nob from my pocket.

'Lovely,' she said.

She wriggled and giggled.

We watched them, black glistening shapes against the black glistening Middens. We heard Grampa:

'Little Helper!'

'Yes, Grampa?' called Mouse.

'Memory! You must show me everything that you does find!'

'OK, Grampa!'

'OK, Little Helper! Get that shovel digging.'

We heard the sucking and slapping as they started to dig. I put my arm around her. She was so small, truly like a little sister. The sky above the city burned. The air was filled with the sound of the flowing river, of distant traffic, of the city's low endless roar. Mouse went to Grampa with something that he'd found in the mud. Grampa held it up to the moon, then slung it far out into the river. Mouse turned back to his digging.

'Heaven Eyes,' I said. 'Do you sometimes think there will be no treasure?'

'Oh, Erin. All them questions you does ask.'

'Do you sometimes think there might be nothing?'

'Him does dig things out every night.'

'But they're not treasures, Heaven Eyes.'

'No, Erin.'

'You do think it. You do sometimes think that there will be no treasures.'

'Yes,' she whispered. 'In mine sleep thoughts I does think that, Erin.'

Mouse found more. He took it to Grampa. Grampa threw it into the river. Mouse went back to his digging. He dug deeper and deeper. The mound of mud beside him grew. We saw him going further down. He stood in a waist-deep hole, then in a chest-deep hole.

'Little Mouse is good as good at the digging,' said Heaven Eyes.

'He is,' I said. 'Be careful, Mouse!' I called.

'Never fear,' said Heaven Eyes. 'Grampa will make sure all is well with his Little Helper.'

I held her gently.

'Tell me about your sleep thoughts, Heaven Eyes,' I whispered. 'Tell me what you see in them.'

'Oh, Erin. These things is secret as secret.'

'Whisper them.'

'These is things that does angry Grampa. These is things that does turn him wild.'

'Whisper them. I am your sister, Heaven Eyes.'

'You will tell nobody nothing?'

'I will tell nobody nothing.'

She held her fingers up to the moon. She breathed deeply.

'In my sleep thoughts I is like a ghost,' she whispered. 'I is with them that is like ghosts.'

'Who are they, Heaven Eyes?'

'No way of telling, Erin. They is close by me. They is holding me and touching me. They is whispering lovely things. They is touching my fingers and whispering lovely lovely things.'

'Can you see their faces?'

'Happy faces. Sweet an kind.'

'What do they look like, Heaven Eyes?'

'The loveliest has hair that is like the sun and eyes that is like the runny water. She has shiny silver on her neck and flowers on her body.'

'What else, Heaven Eyes?'

'There is another further out. I cannot eye him proper. Him is shadowed like under the printing press. And there is others, sometimes little, sometimes big. And I cannot eye these proper either. They is little figures, like the ghosts across the runny water. But they is smiling and laughing.'

She gasped and nibbled a Hob Nob.

'You must say nothing about these things,' she said.

'I will say nothing.'

She sighed. We watched Mouse digging down.

'The loveliest is that lovely, Erin. She does make me cry sometimes in my sleeping.'

'What does she whisper, Heaven Eyes?'

'Little words and whisperings. She does tell me I is lovely.'

'Does she call you Heaven Eyes?'

'No, Erin.'

'What does she call you?'

Her voice grew smaller, became the quietest whisper.

'Tell nobody,' she said.

'Nobody.'

'She does whisper Anna, Anna, little Anna.'

'Anna? That's your name?'

'My name is Heaven Eyes. Anna is my name in sleeping time. Anna is my fibbing and imagining name. Anna is the name that must never get telt to nobody, specially to Grampa.'

She gripped my hand.

'You must not tell him of these things, Erin.'

'Have you told him?'

'Once way back. Way way back. He did say these things was lies and wrongnesses. He was wild, Erin. Wild as wild. You must not tell him nothing. Nothing.'

'Nothing,' I whispered.

I held her tight. I thought of all the other questions I wanted to ask. The moon shone down. Mouse and Grampa dug and glistened. The mud sucked and splashed.

'Heaven . . .' I said.

'Don't ask nothing more, Erin.'

'But Heaven Eyes . . .'

And I was about to ask her more, when a scream came from below us. Mouse slithered and scrambled from his hole. He ran across the Black Middens. He shouted my name again and again. He screamed. He ran across the raft, climbed the ladder. He came over the edge. He trembled, gasped, howled my name. Water and mud splashed down from him.

'Erin! Erin!'

I jumped up and got hold of him.

'Mouse! What is it, Mouse?'

His mouth gaped and his eyes were wild.

'A body!' he yelled. 'There's a body in the Middens, Erin.'

He shuddered and wept.

Below us, Grampa leaned on his shovel and gazed up through the moonlight at us.

Nineteen

'Murder!' said January.

We huddled together on the quay. Heaven Eyes stood frantic at our side.

'Murder!' he said.

He took out his knife and gripped it in his fist.

'Murder!' he said. 'That's what his secret is. Bloody murder!'

We stared down at the Middens. Grampa stood above the hole that Mouse had made. He stepped down into it and the blackness of his body was taken into the blackness of the Middens.

'What was it like?' said January.

Mouse gasped and jabbered.

'A body. A body. I felt it there. Thought it was something. Put my hand in the mud. Felt fingers there. Felt a hand sticking up. Saw it shining in the moonlight. Like it was reaching up at me, but icy cold an still.'

'Still as still,' I whispered.

'Still as still, Erin.'

'What else?' said January. 'What about the face?'

Mouse gaped at him.

'A face? Didn't want to see no face. Didn't want to . . .'

'He's coming!' I hissed.

We looked down. He splashed over the Middens, carrying the shovels and buckets.

January reached out and grabbed Heaven by the throat.

'Murder!' he spat into her face. 'Murder! Who has Grampa murdered, Heaven Eyes?'

Tears streamed down her face. She reached out to me.

'Erin! Erin!'

I pulled her from him.

'The axe!' he said. 'The axe beside the desk. Come on!'

We hurried through the pitch-black alleys to the printing works. Heaven sobbed and sobbed.

'You is wrong!' she whimpered. 'Erin, tell Janry Carr that Janry Carr is wrong!'

We rushed beneath the outstretched wings to the office. I saw January's footprints on the shelves. Objects that had been on the shelves were scattered on the floor. January grabbed the axe. I took his knife. Mouse and Heaven cried. We stood and waited.

'Mebbe he's done in lots of kids like us that's come here,' said January.

He glared at Heaven.

'Speak!' he said. 'How many kids has Grampa fettled? How many has he killed?'

She sheltered at my back.

January cursed and spat. He stared at me. He caught his breath.

'Her family,' he said. 'What happened to her family?'

I gripped the knife.

'Dunno,' I said. 'I don't know.'

We watched each other.

'It can't be,' I whispered.

'Can't it?'

He dug into his pocket. He showed a photograph. It was cracked and creased. It was a family – mother, father, children – smiling out at us. The mother had blonde hair, blue eyes, she wore a brightly coloured floral summer frock. She held a baby in her arms. I couldn't speak. My heart thundered and my head roared. I held the photograph to my face. I tried to see the baby's fingers. Then Heaven was at my side. She caught the edge of the picture with her webbed hands.

'Erin,' she whispered. 'Oh, Erin. This is my sleep thoughts, Erin.'

I let her take it from me. She squatted on the floor and gazed at it in wonder.

'It's from up there,' said January. He nodded upwards to the ceiling. His eyes widened. 'That's it! He's done them all in! Bloody murder!'

'No,' I said.

'Ask her.'

I stared at Heaven Eyes, who trembled on the floor.

'Anna,' I whispered.

'Not that name, Erin.'

'Anna. Anna. What else do you see in your sleep thoughts?'

'Nothing! Nothing nothing nothing! That Janry Carr is all lies and fibs and wrongnesses!'

She jumped at him with her fingers spread like claws. He shoved her off. She sprawled on the office floor. He spat and cursed. He glared at me.

'You,' he said. 'You're the one that made us stay with these freaks and crazies. So you better make sure you help me to do him in.'

We stood there, gasping, whimpering, listening.

Then the sound of Grampa's footsteps came out of the night and approached the door.

Twenty

He came in dripping mud and water, black as night. His shoulders were huge. He dropped the shovels and buckets and they clattered to the floor. He stood stock-still, staring at January with the axe raised above his head, at me with the knife gripped in my fist and pointed towards him.

'Heaven!' he hissed.

'Grampa!'

'You is all right, Heaven?'

'Yes, Grampa.'

Suddenly the carving knife was in his hand.

'Come to me, my little one,' he said. 'Come away from them ghosts.'

She stood up to go to him. I caught her arm and held her tight.

'She's ours,' said January.

He stepped forward, holding the axe. Grampa stepped back, into the doorway.

'Touch her and you is dead,' he said.

He narrowed his eyes.

'Little Helper,' he said.

Mouse shuddered and whimpered.

'Little Helper!'

'Grampa.'

'You is all right, Little Helper?'

'He's terrified,' I whispered.

'Touch him an you is dead,' said Grampa.

'Murderer!' hissed January. 'Murderer!'

Grampa wiped the slithery mud from his eyes and stared at him. He held his hand out.

'Come, Heaven Eyes,' he said.

I held her tight.

'Keep still, sister,' I hissed. 'Keep still, Anna.'

I closed my eyes.

'Mum!' I whispered. 'Mum! Mum!'

Her voice rose inside me.

'Stay calm, Erin. Stay calm and everything will be well.'

'He does not want to hurt you,' said Heaven Eyes. 'Grampa is a good Grampa. He will do no harm.'

I heard January's frantic breath, his terror, his excitement. His arm holding the axe jerked and trembled. Grampa wiped the mud from his eyes and stepped forward.

'Grampa!' said Mouse.

'Little Helper?'

'Grampa, there was a body in the Middens. A body buried deep deep down.'

'I do know this, Little Helper. And that is why there is great joy in your digging this night.'

'Great joy?'

'Great joy, my little helper. For you has found a saint this night. You has found a saint that in all his years of digging Grampa has never never found.'

He reached out his hand.

'Come to me,' he whispered. 'Come away with little Heaven Eyes from these wicked ghosts and I will tell you all about saints.'

He glared at me, at January.

'I has seen,' he whispered. 'I has seen how you has led my Heaven Eyes astray. I has seen how you has led my Little Helper astray. These two is precious. Time for you to go. Time to leave them here alone and safe with Grampa.'

'We won't leave without them,' I said.

He stepped forward suddenly. He snatched the axe easily from January's grip. He knocked the knife from my hand. He took Mouse and Heaven in his arms.

'What now?' he whispered. 'Does you leave alone, or does Grampa have to fettle you?'

He shoved Mouse and Heaven into the space behind the desk. He came at January and me. He had the axe in one hand, the carving knife in the other. We backed towards the door.

'Grampa!' said Heaven Eyes. 'Do not touch them. These is my friends, Grampa!'

'Friends!' he hissed. 'These is ghosts that's putting wrongness in your head, my little one. Tell them go, and leave us here happy, safe and alone.'

Heaven wept. Her eyes shone with pain, with love for all of us.

'But Grampa! This is mine sister that you is sending away.'

'You has no sisters! You has nothing! You has only Grampa and now Grampa's Little Helper!'

She sobbed. Mouse put his arm around her.

'Grampa,' she called. 'Oh, Grampa!' She held up the photograph. 'What is this picture of mine sleep thoughts? Who is these ghosts? What happened to mine Mum and mine Dad? What happened to mine sisters and brothers?'

He stopped. His body slumped. He rolled his eyes. He stared at me but spoke to Heaven.

'What did you say, my little one?'

'What happened to them, Grampa? Mine Mum, mine Dad, mine brothers, mine sisters?'

Mud and water trickled across his eyes.

'Does you see?' he whispered. 'Does you see what you has done to lovely Heaven Eyes?'

And he dropped the axe and the knife and went to her. He took her in his arms and they cried together and spoke each other's name time and time and time again.

Twenty-One

January and I stood silent. We watched them for a time. The tall old man dripping black mud, sobbing, holding the delicate Heaven Eyes in his huge arms. Mouse crouching against the wall, filthy too, staring in dread and fascination. The shovels, the buckets, the shelves of treasures, the boxes of secrets, the great book, the knives and the axe. Soon we left them there. We beckoned Mouse, stepped out into the printing works, and closed the door on them.

January rubbed his eyes.

'Is this happening?' he whispered.

'Yes. It's happening.'

'And there really was a body?'

'Yes,' said Mouse.

We shuddered and wondered. We roamed between the angels and the eagles. Bats flickered against the starry sky. Moonlight poured down.

'There were other things,' said January. 'Lots of things. Newspapers and photographs, scribbled pages, drawings, trinkets. The boxes are filled with them.'

'Treasures,' I said. 'Stuff from her past.'

'Yes. Treasures. I'd just found them when I heard Mouse screaming.'

We stood in silence beneath the moon, stunned by this place we'd come to, by what we'd found here.

'We could just leave,' said January. 'Just go back to the raft and sail away from it all.'

'We can't,' I said.

'Yes,' he said. 'I know that.'

We sat down in the doorway of the printing works and looked out across the river. Soon Mouse curled up and slept. January laughed.

'Look at him. It's like he's right at home here. He can sleep anywhere, any time.'

'Dormouse, eh?' I said.

We leaned on each other.

'I keep on dreaming that you've gone,' I said. 'I see you all alone going out to sea.'

'I've almost done it. Climb down to the raft, jump aboard, set off all alone. Seems easy.'

'But you haven't.'

'Mebbe it's because I can't.'

He shrugged.

'I can't leave you, Erin.'

We stared into each other's eyes.

'I know that,' I said. 'And you know that one day I'll go anywhere with you. Anywhere. I'll go to the edge of death with you. You know that, don't you?'

'Yes,' he said. 'I know that, Erin.'

We watched the river glittering beneath the stars. Both of us became lost in ourselves, in our memories, our mysteries and dreams. I slipped into the little garden in St Gabriel's and felt Mum's arms around me. Where was January? In a cardboard box, maybe, wrapped in blankets, being carried through a bitter winter's night.

We were silent for a long time. The moon journeyed across the sky. The noise of distant traffic came to us, the noise of distant music.

I felt how January's spirit had quietened, how his anger, his fear and his agitation had faded.

'Erin,' he whispered.

'Yes.'

'Do you think that one day we'll know everything there is to know about ourselves?'

I thought of the beautiful terrified young woman rushing from the hospital steps into the deep winter dark. I thought of a man on a boat that danced down the river and out into the sea.

'I don't know,' I said. I held his arm. 'There'll always be lots of things we don't know. But maybe one day when you least expect it, your Mum will come along and say, "Hello, I'm your Mum." '

'Yes,' he said. 'She will.'

'Yes.'

He sat up straight and faced me.

'She still loves me and wants me, Erin. One day she'll come back for me.'

Then he slumped and leaned against me.

'I've got nothing, you know,' he said.

'Nothing?'

'No treasures. No photographs. No earrings. No lipsticks. Nothing. Not even a memory. Just dreams and stupid thoughts and stupid hopes.'

'You've got your friends.'

'Maybe.'

'You have. You've got friends that love you.'

He trembled as he cried.

'Sometimes,' he said. 'I want to hate everybody. I want to hate them and hurt them and make them hate me.'

I smiled.

'I know that,' I said. 'But you can't bring yourself to hate them.'

'No. Can't even manage that.'

We were silent again. Mum came to us. I felt her breath on my cheek. She put her arms around me and around January and we sat together in the moonlight, half-sleeping, half-waking, lost in the joy and fear of being alive in this mysterious world.

Twenty-Two

And then dawn came, and the stars faded, and pigeons and sparrows took the place of bats above us. Gulls screamed over the river. We looked at each other in surprise. We smiled. We stood up. We gently shook Mouse awake.

'God knows what's been happening back there,' Jan said.

We went back to the office. There was silence inside. We opened the door gently. Grampa sat with Heaven Eyes on the floor. He had his arm around her. There were opened boxes beside them. Heaven Eyes held a photograph in her webbed fingers.

'Erin,' she said. 'I did think you had gone off with Janry Carr.'

Her eyes were bright, burning, filled with tears.

'Oh, Erin,' she said.

She turned to Grampa and he nodded and lowered his eyes.

I crouched beside her. She turned the photograph to me. It was crumpled and faded, but I could see the family there: mother, father, four children sitting before them. She lifted it closer to my eyes.

'Eye close as close,' she said. 'And you will see a tiny Heaven Eyes.'

I looked closely. The tiniest of the three. She was fair-haired, bright-eyed, pale-cheeked. She had tiny hands with webs between the fingers. There were webs between her tiny toes. She sat on the woman's lap and the woman's hands were tenderly holding her.

'Is me,' said Heaven Eyes.

'Is you.'

'I cannot mouth much, Erin.'

'You don't need to mouth.'

I looked at Grampa.

'It is her?' I asked.

'Yes,' he said. 'Is Heaven Eyes.'

His eyes were filled with his memories, with his mysteries, with his confusions.

'All has been wrongness,' he said. 'All has been imagining.'

Heaven ran her fingers across herself as she was, across her mother, her father, her sister, her brothers.

'My name is Anna,' said Heaven Eyes.

She bit her lip at the name, Anna.

'Anna,' she whispered. 'Anna. Anna. It does feel that funny in my mouth. Anna. Anna.'

'You were a lovely little baby,' I said.

January took the photograph and stared at it.

'You were,' he said. 'You were lovely, Anna.'

'I was not a fishy froggy thing deep down in the black Black Middens.'

'No. You were a fishy froggy thing like me, growing deep inside your Mum.'

She took the photograph again. She touched the woman's face. She was sheepish, joyous, terrified.

'Is my Mum,' she whispered. 'Is my Dad. Is my brothers and my sister.'

There were other photographs. Each of them was faded, cracked, bleached, like they'd been lost in water. They showed the same people, differently arranged. One showed them in a living room, heaped up and giggling on a sofa. There were pictures of just the children, of just the parents. There was a picture of the parents on their wedding day, she in her white gown and veil, he in black, both of them grinning out. One showed the family on a little sailing boat, gathered around the mast. They wore waterproofs and life jackets, even tiny Anna. The wind whipped at their hair and the sea danced behind them.

We gazed into the photographs, into Anna's past.

'You were very happy,' I said.

'Is true.'

She held my arm.

'But my mind is flapping like a pigeon's wing and swirling like the runny water and dancing like the dust. I does not know if I am happy now.'

'You had a lovely Mum,' I said. 'You had a lovely Dad. You had lovely brothers and a lovely sister. Anyone would give anything to have these things. These are your treasures, Anna. You have found your treasures.'

She touched her Mum's face.

'Mum,' she whispered. 'Mum. Mum.'

Grampa lowered his head. Tears trickled from his eyes.

'I has been wrong,' he said. 'All was for you, little one. All was to keep you happy forever in your heart. And look at the tears that is running from you now.'

'And from you, Grampa.'

She reached out to him, and she hugged him, and they rocked in each other's arms.

I lifted a newspaper from one of the boxes. It came from ten years ago. A headline told of a whole family lost at sea. January cursed. We put it back in the box and just looked at each other.

'The body,' said Jan at last. 'We'd better find it again.'

'You're joking,' I said, but knew that he wasn't.

Twenty-Three

Mouse stayed in the office with Grampa and Heaven Eyes as we moved out.

'You're crazy,' I said.

'Aye,' said Jan. 'You're always saying that.'

He grinned like a devil.

'Where's your spirit of adventure, eh?'

I laughed and thumped his arm.

'I'm glad you haven't gone away alone,' I said.

'Me, too.'

I smiled.

'Let's go adventuring,' I said.

'Yes. Me and you.'

I shuddered and grinned.

'Me and you,' I said. 'Me and you and the body and the Middens.'

We left the printing works. Jan turned towards the quay. The sun was already up, glaring low in the east above the hidden sea.

'What if it was murder?' I said.

'D'you think it was?'

'Look at him last night and he'd do anything to protect Heaven Eyes.'

'Then it's murder.'

'So what would we do?'

'Do?'

'Well, the police. You've got to do something about murder.'

'He'd call it fettling.'

'Whatever he called it, it would still be murder.'

'Hell's teeth, Erin. Let's just find out first, then think what to do.'

We came to the quay. Since last night's digging, the tide had come in and gone out again. The raft rested on the mud. The holes in the Middens had been smoothed out. Over on the other side of the river, a couple of early-morning joggers bounced along the cycle track. Jan laughed.

'Ghosts, eh?'' he said.

We looked down. Jan muttered, trying to work out exactly where Mouse had been digging last night.

'We'll never find the right spot,' I said.

'Giving up?' he said.

'Course not.'

I shrugged.

'We'll find it. Come on.'

He stepped down on to the ancient ladder. I followed him. He led me out towards the water, towards the edge of the dry land, to where our feet started to slither and sink into the soft surface.

'Round about here, I reckon,' he said.

I stared at him.

He laughed.

'Come on, Little Helper,' he said. 'Get that shovel digging!'

We started to dig. We lifted great spadefuls of oily, silty, stinking mud and water. Our shovels slopped and sucked. Within seconds we were filthy. We slithered down into the holes we dug. We were ankle-deep, shin-deep, knee-deep. We heaped up mounds of the stuff at our sides. We dug deeper, deeper. I looked across at Jan and he whooped and was like a crazed black creature made of the mud itself. The sun rose higher and the morning grew warmer and the stench of oil and rot and waste intensified. We gagged. We spat out mouthfuls of silt. It gathered in our eyes, in our ears, in the creases on our skin. I asked myself what I was doing. I told myself that Mouse was mistaken, that there was no body, that there was nothing here but the stones and broken pottery and lumps of rubbish that we found and flung away. I told myself we should just go back to the office and try to get Heaven Eyes to leave with us. Or we should go to the police and bring them here and get them to sort out the mystery. We should do anything but dig in the filthy Black Middens for a body that was the last thing in the world I wanted to find. But I dug and spat and wiped my face and dug deeper, deeper till I was sick of it all and was just about to tell Jan that I was giving up when I saw the tips of the fingers in the black black mud.

I scrambled out of the hole. I stared up river to the real world, to the bridge with the glittering traffic moving across it, to the rooftops and spires of the roaring city.

'Erin!'

I swung my head to him.

He scrambled, slithered out of his own digging.

'Erin?'

I nodded. I couldn't look down.

'Yes,' I whispered. 'Yes.'

He knelt there.

'Where?' he said.

'There. In there.'

He slithered in. He lifted mud from the bottom of the hole with his hands. And I knew by his groans that he had found it.

Twenty-Four

'It's not real,' he said.

'Eh?'

It's not real. It's a model or a statue or something. It's made of leather or wood or something. It's not a body. It's not real.'

He was out of the hole again, kneeling beside.

'Go on,' he said. 'Go on down and see for yourself. '

I still couldn't look down.

'Go on, Erin,' he said.

I took a deep breath and went back down. Now a whole hand was exposed. It was half-submerged in the mud. It glistened beneath the sun. I saw the loops and whorls on the fingertips, the lines crossing the palm. I touched, and yes it was like some kind of leather, something not skin and flesh and bone. The hand rested there, as if waiting for a gift, an offering, for something to be placed on to it.

'See?' said Jan.

'Yes.'

I dug around the hand with my own hand. I exposed a

forearm, an elbow, all covered in the smooth, delicate, leather-like skin. It glistened in the sunlight. I stared, and saw how beautiful it was, so life-like, but like a copy of life, left here in the Black Middens waiting for someone like January and me to find it. I scraped away more mud. An upper arm, a shoulder, a chest, a beautifully formed ribcage with the strange skin draped over it. Jan watched and gasped. I turned to him.

'What did Grampa mean?' I whispered. 'What did he mean by saying it was a saint?'

His eyes were wide. I saw that he too was entranced by this beautiful thing emerging from the Middens.

'Dunno, Erin.'

I pushed more mud away. There were fragments of some fabric resting on the body. They broke up and came away with the mud. A fragment of metal, a catch or something. I held it in my fingers, held it up to the sun, passed it up to Jan. I found little coins in the mud. I wiped them and passed them up to Jan. I found another catch resting on his chest and passed it up to Jan.

'What is it?' he said. 'What have we found, Erin?'

I kept on lifting away the mud. I paused. I prayed. I whispered to Mum. Then I lifted the mud from where the face should be.

His head rested in the black mud. The cheeks were sunken, the eyes were closed. The lips formed a calm straight line. Black hair was tangled on his brow. The face shone, reflecting the light. It was still as still, still as still, but it rested there in the mud facing the sun as if it was waiting, as if at any moment the eyes might simply open and gaze into mine. I ran my fingertips across the beautiful face. I knew now that it wasn't a model or a statue. It was a dead man who had been lost for many years in the Black Middens, who had been preserved by the silt and oil. It was a beautiful young man from a long time past.

I climbed up to January.

'It is a man,' I whispered. 'It's just that he hasn't rotted away.'

We looked down.

'We should be terrified,' I said.

'I know.'

'But he's lovely, isn't he?'

Jan smiled, shook his head.

'Lovely as lovely, eh?'

'What should we do?'

'God knows, Erin.'

We rubbed the clasps and the coins and looked at them.

'Not ages past,' said January. 'Maybe a hundred years, something like that.'

'Not murdered by Grampa.'

'Not murdered by Grampa.'

He stared at the empty river running past.

'Probably the time when the river was full,' he said. 'Loads of ships. Loads of men working on the quays and in the shipyards. Maybe he just fell into the water and nobody knew until it was too late.'

'Maybe they searched for weeks and couldn't find him. They thought he was at the bottom of the river or washed out to sea.'

January stared at the clasps.

'They're from overalls,' he said. 'That's what they are. They were to fasten his overalls.'

'A working man,' I said.

'A working man.'

We looked at the banks of the river, the places where the warehouses and workplaces had gone. The banks opposite were landscaped and turfed. There were footpaths and cycle tracks. Up river there were wastelands, dilapidated quays, all waiting to be cleared, too. There were new pubs and clubs where there used to be great cranes and loading bays. Behind us were more ruined workplaces, the printing works, all waiting to be demolished and swept away. We looked down again at the beautiful young man in the mud, the man from an age that had been wiped away.

'He'd have children,' I said. 'He'd have a wife. They'd be waiting for him to come home again, and he wouldn't come.'

'Who was he?'

'No way of knowing.'

'A mystery.'

'What should we do?'

'We could leave him. We could cover him again. We could bring him out.'

We said nothing else. We slithered down together and

carefully uncovered him. We worked slowly, gently. We eased our hands under his body and loosened him from the Middens. We smiled to see that his leather boots, preserved like his body, still clung to his feet. We lifted him, carried and dragged him up to the dry land. We thought he would be stiff and awkward, but his body arched as we raised him. There was still a looseness in his joints. We laid him on the raft, facing the sky. We crouched beside him and ran our hands across his skin. We touched his face, stroked his brow. We arranged his hair tidily on his head. We scooped handfuls of water from the river and washed the mud from him. Moment by moment he became more life-like, more beautiful. Then we lifted him between us and carried him up the ancient ladder to the quay.

Twenty-Five

We took him to the Ouseburn and washed him clean. We washed the Middens from ourselves. We cleared a space of litter and laid him on the printing floor, close to the office, beneath the outstretched wings of an angel. We arranged the coins and clasps beside his head. We laid out his name in metal letters at his side:

The sAiNT

As we worked, the sun rose higher. It streamed down on to him through the ruined rafters and the dancing dust. A hidden bird began singing somewhere in the works. The man lay there as if he was sleeping, as if at any moment he might open his eyes, stretch his arms and legs, sit up, and take his place in the world again.

It was the afternoon before we went back into the office. Heaven Eyes and Mouse still gazed at Heaven's treasures. Grampa sat above them at his desk, turning back the pages of his great book.

'Come and see,' we said.

We led Mouse and Heaven through the alleyways between the ancient machines and showed him lying there.

'Who is he?' they whispered.

'A mystery,' we said. 'A working man.'

They stared, in dread and fascination.

Then Grampa came. He walked slowly, with the filth of the Middens still clinging to him. He eased himself to the floor and he knelt there, looking at the dead man.

'Great joy,' he said. 'Great joy, Little Helper. You has truly found a saint.'

'A saint?' said Mouse.

'There is secrets and there is treasures and there is saints waiting to be found. These saints is them from way back, way way way back in the past, afore Grampa, afore Heaven Eyes, afore us all.'

He looked at Mouse. He reached out and touched his cheek.

'One day way back I did hear that such saints was waiting to be discovered in these Middens. But it did take one like you, with great goodness in his heart, to find one. I must thank you, Little Helper, for finding this saint in the deep deep dark and bringing him to me.'

He closed his eyes. Perhaps he prayed. My head reeled as I looked at this strange circle around this figure on the printing floor below the ruined roof. I told myself that I was dreaming, hallucinating. This is impossible, I whispered to myself. Then I remembered Wilson Cairns' words just before he ran away: It's possible. It's possible. I thought of the way his eyes stared through us to a stunning place beyond. I thought of his last words: Keep watching. I watched. And then from somewhere outside us there came a great roaring and clanking, like some huge machine was coming near.

Grampa reached out to Heaven Eyes.

'I has been a good Grampa?' he whispered.

She clung to him.

'You is a lovely Grampa,' she said.

'You has seen your treasures now.'

'Yes, Grampa.'

'I has hidden many things from you.'

'Yes, Grampa. Many many things.'

'And there is still many things waiting to be shown.'

He turned his eyes to me.

'Your friend does understand,' he said.

'Yes,' I said. 'I understand, Grampa.'

He sighed and lowered his head.

'Heaven Eyes?' he whispered.

'Yes, Grampa?'

'Is there great wrongness in this hiding things?'

'There is no wrongness, Grampa. You is Caretaker. You is been only trying to take care.'

He sighed.

'Yes, little one. I is Caretaker. I has been only trying to take care.'

He sighed again, deeply. He looked old, so old. He looked at me, at January, at Mouse.

'These is your brothers and sisters, Heaven Eyes? These is

your brothers and sisters come back to you again?'

Heaven Eyes whispered.

'Will you be my brother, Mouse Gullane?'

'Yes,' said Mouse.

'Will you be my brother, Janry Carr?'

'Yes,' said January.

'Yes,' said Heaven Eyes. 'These is my sister and my brothers come back to me, Grampa.'

'Lovely,' he said. 'Lovely as lovely.'

He focused on my eyes.

'You will now take care of Heaven Eyes?'

'Yes. We will now take care of Heaven Eyes.'

'And will you tell her the things that needs to be telt?'

'Yes.'

Tears trickled down the black mud on his cheeks.

'There is also truth,' he said. 'There is truth that I did find you lying on the black Black Middens in the moony night, my little one. There is truth that I did bring you out and care for you.' He lowered his eyes. 'I did find your little treasures with you, wrapped inside your pocket, and I did keep them hid from you, my Heaven Eyes. I did think that this would keep you happy in your heart.'

'And I always has been happy, Grampa. Happy as happy.'

He stroked her cheek. He reached down and stroked the saint's cheek.

He whispered, quiet as quiet.

'Mebbe now the time is come when you must cross the runny water to the world of ghosts, my little one.'

'Oh Grampa,' she said. 'Oh my Grampa.'

They held each other tight.

I lifted my head and listened. Not too far away, the great clanking and roaring intensified.

Twenty-Six

I went by myself through the ancient alleyways. I walked away from the river, went beyond the printing works, through the ruins of warehouses and sheds and factories and offices. I scrambled across collapsed walls, beneath teetering roofs. I leapt across great cracks and potholes. I read faded signs telling of metalworkers, shipwrights, ropemakers, bootmakers, coal merchants, ship's suppliers, nail and screw and wire manufacturers, tea importers, spice importers. Rats scuttled here. Mangy dogs watched timidly from shadows. Skinny cats hissed and arched their backs and bared their teeth. Pigeons flapped and cooed. Crows scavenged. Outside it all was the city's low deep endless din, and nearby the roaring, the clanking. And then I saw it, the huge crane making its way towards this place from the city's edge. I sheltered in a doorway and watched it come. It moved slowly, gracelessly. The ground cracked beneath its great metal tread. A huge metal ball dangled from its jib. It squealed to a halt fifty yards away from me. A young man in jeans and T-shirt and a red helmet jumped down from the cab on to the metal tread. He lit a fag, pulled a newspaper from his pocket, sprawled there in the sunshine and waited. I watched. I waited too. And then the next crane loomed out from the city's edge and ground its way towards us.

I hurried back to the printing works. In the office, Grampa was in his uniform. He scribbled in his great book. He murmured about the saint, about the great treasure found by Mouse Gullane in the black Black Middens. Heaven Eyes and Mouse were feasting on Milk Tray and Hob Nobs. January knelt on the floor. He had a heap of Grampa's notebooks, a little pile of newspapers. He was placing them into one of the boxes from the high shelves.

'Where you been?' he said.

'It's all going to be cleared away,' I said.

I told him what I'd seen, what I expected.

'Can't be today,' he said. 'Too late to start today.'

'No. But tomorrow.'

We looked at Heaven Eyes and Grampa.

'What can we do?' he whispered.

I shook my head. We shared a packet of Hob Nobs. We listened. We watched the door. We expected workmen to come in at any moment, wearing hard helmets. They didn't come. The afternoon wore on.

'And Heaven's brothers and sister is come back to her at last,' Grampa murmured as he wrote. 'And they will take her cross the runny water to the world of ghosts.' He scribbled on, he murmured on. Soon his hand began to slow. 'And Grampa's taking care is done,' he whispered. 'Love. Grampa an Heaven Eyes. Love, love, love . . .'

The pencil fell from his fingers to the book.

He looked down at Heaven Eyes.

'Lovely,' he whispered. 'Lovely as lovely.'

Then he closed his eyes and lowered his head to the book.

'Grampa,' said Heaven Eyes, turning suddenly to him. 'Grampa. My Grampa!'

And she leapt to him.

But Grampa was still. Still as still.

Twenty-Seven

Everything would go. The printing works, the warehouses, the factories, the offices and sheds. The great printing machines bearing eagles and angels would be put into a museum. The rubble would be hauled away. The ground would be broken up and bulldozed. Shining new offices would appear. There'd be pubs and clubs and restaurants. There'd be turf and little hills with plaques showing how things had been. There'd be cycle tracks and walkways. There'd be jetties where little sailing boats would be tethered. The sun would shine down and this beautiful new place would glisten beneath it, beside a glistening blue river and people would wander at ease on broad pathways. We saw it all, January, Mouse and I, late that afternoon, when we left Heaven Eyes alone with Grampa for a time. We saw it on the great billboards that had been put up beside the waiting cranes. We stood there and wondered, lost in the mystery of Grampa and his death, the mystery of the saint, the mystery of this new world that would soon appear.

When we went back to her, she sat on the floor beside her

box of treasures. She was calm and smiling.

'He did tell me this,' she said. 'He did tell me that one day he would be still as still and I must cross the runny water.'

She held my hand.

'How did you know that this was the time to come for me?' she asked.

'I don't know how we knew,' I said. 'It was January who made his raft and made us come.'

'Janry Carr,' she said. 'Janry Carr, my brother.'

We didn't know what to do with Grampa. He lay there on his book. We laid his pencils beside him. We tidied his shovels and buckets. As evening came on, we lit candles and placed them near him. We said prayers. We said that he was a good Grampa, that he had truly taken care.

I sat with Heaven Eyes with my arm around her.

'Grampa is gone,' she said.

'Yes, Heaven Eyes.'

'He is gone but he will keep staying in my heart.'

'Yes, Heaven Eyes.'

'And I will cry much for him, but I will be happy for him in my heart.'

We looked at her photographs, her family.

'You must whisper, "Mum. Mum",' I told her.

'Why is this?' she asked.

'Just try,' I said. 'Mum. Mum.'

She took a deep breath.

'Mum,' she whispered. 'Mum. Mum.'

She bit her lip.

'Does feel that funny in my mouth,' she said. 'Mum. Mum.'

'Just whisper it,' I said. 'Just try it, Anna.'

Her Mum smiled out of the photograph at us.

'Is a lovely Mum,' said Heaven Eyes.

'Yes,' I said.

'Mum. Mum.'

'Say it gentle as gentle,' I said.

'Mum. Mum.'

I felt her spirit relaxing, and I felt the new excitement entering her.

'What is this new funniness in mine head?' she said.

'Funniness?'

'Funniness when I whisper, "Mum. Mum".'

I smiled at her.

'Mebbe this is your Mum,' I said. 'Mebbe she's finding a way back into your heart and into your head.'

'Oh, Erin. She is whispering to me.'

'She whispers, "Anna. Anna".'

'Yes, Erin. She does whisper, "Anna. Anna", just like in my sleep thoughts.'

'But these are not sleep thoughts.'

'No Erin. These is waking thoughts and thoughts as bright as day.'

Twenty-Eight

Deep into the night. Deep into the dark. The moon poured down through the broken rafters. No one slept, but our minds trembled, drifting through truth and dreams and imagination. Jan and I nibbled Hob Nobs and orange creams and wandered over the printing floor. We talked about the raft and about tomorrow.

'We'll have to leave Grampa and the saint here,' he said. 'We'll have to leave them for the workmen to find.'

'No room on the raft,' I said.

'No room on the raft.'

We put candles around the man we'd dug out from the Middens and we sat with him.

'What will they say,' I said, 'when they find them here?'

He smiled.

'All kinds of weird tales'll be told, eh?'

'Can't wait to read them,' I said.

I picked at the metal letters on the floor. I laid out the name:

HeaVEn eYeS

'That's the story they won't be able to tell,' I said.

'It's our story,' said Jan.

'That's right. Even the bits that we don't know and the bits we'll never get to know.'

'Truth and dreams and bits made up.'

We laughed.

'Wonder what Heaven'll put in her Life Story book,' said Jan.

He told me about the newspapers.

'There are names for all of them,' he said. 'The mother, the father, the sister, the brothers. Their boat was washed up on a beach. No bodies were ever found. The whole family was lost at sea.'

'Except Anna.'

'Except Anna.'

'Washed into the river on the tide, washed on to the Black Middens, found by Grampa.'

'We'll tell her what we know of her story.'

'But slowly.'

'Yes. Very slowly.'

Our minds drifted, drifted, drifted.

I thought it was just the candles, the way their light flickered across his skin. I squeezed my eyes. I thought it was exhaustion. I thought it was the effect of seeing Grampa die, the effect of all the events of the last few days. I squeezed my eyes. I shook my head. The movement was tiny, almost invisible, a gentle flexing of his fingers, a gentle arching of his back. Then nothing. It must have been the candles, my exhaustion. Then it came again, both hands flexing, that gentle arching of his back. The saint slowly raised his knees and lowered them again.

'Jan,' I breathed. 'January.'

'No,' he whispered.

'Yes,' I breathed.

He was so beautiful, the way he turned on the floor, the way he raised himself and crouched there in front of us. He glowed, reflecting candlelight and moonlight. He made no sound. His eyes didn't open. His lips still formed the straight calm line. He stood up, and he was slender and graceful. He paused, as if he was waiting.

We heard Heaven's cry from inside the office:

'Grampa! Mine Grampa!'

What was it that came out of the office? It wasn't Grampa's body. That stayed there, resting across the book and the desk. Mouse told us later that something in the exact shape of Grampa moved out of the body and went to the door. Heaven said it was Grampa's goodness, Grampa's heart. What Jan and I saw was a shape as tall as Grampa, but it was blurred and translucent. It flowed rather than walked across the printing floor. The saint waited, then led the shape from the printing works into the alleyways and towards the quay. We followed. Heaven held my hand. We came to the broken ground above the Middens. The saint went down first, then Grampa's shape. We leaned over the edge. They walked side by side across the Black Middens. There was no slithering of feet, no sinking. They moved over the Midden's edge, where the water and the land mingle, and they entered the river. By the light of the moon, we saw them going down, side by side, until the water had covered them and there were just eddies and sparkling ripples and the tide running down towards the sea.

Twenty-Nine

Heaven Eyes kissed his cheek. She whispered that she loved him and he would stay forever in her heart. She shed some tears.

'Bye bye, Grampa,' she said. 'Bye bye, my lovely Grampa.' January, Mouse and I touched him gently. I rested my hand on his book and turned to Heaven. She helped me to slide it from beneath him. We packed it with his other books and her treasures in one of the boxes. We packed the rucksacks and made our way across the printing floor. We collected letters as we walked, enough letters for all our names and the names of all our stories, and put them in our pockets. We ate Hob Nobs and orange creams. We walked through the alleyways to the bright sunlight that poured down on to the quay. We sat there on the edge. We watched the tide flowing in, inching its way over the black Black Middens.

Traffic glittered on the bridges. Cyclists and walkers moved across the opposite bank. Seagulls screamed.

'We could do anything, you know,' said January. 'We could go anywhere. We don't have to go back.'

We smelt the distant sea. The distant moors were dark against the sky. The sky was brilliant blue, going on forever.

'I know that,' I said.

'But mebbe we should get Heaven sorted first. Then we can all clear off again.'

We laughed.

'Let's walk next time,' I said.

'Aye. Let's walk next time.'

Mouse let Squeak tumble through his fingers.

'Can I come?' he whispered.

'No!' snapped January. He laughed again. 'Aye,' he said. 'How'll we ever manage now without the Little Helper?'

The water reached the raft and began to lift it.

'I is feared,' said Heaven Eyes.

'Me, too,' I said. 'We are always in fear. But we are also brave.'

'Brave as brave,' she said.

'Yes. Brave as brave.'

We went over the edge, carried the sacks and treasures down, put them in the middle of the raft. We took down new oars made of snapped timber. Behind us, there was a great roaring and clanking of machines. We saw men in brightly coloured hard hats in the alleyways. We heard voices calling. Jan held the rope as we leapt across the running water on to the raft. Then he untied the rope and jumped aboard, and the tide helped carry us free of the Middens, and we pressed our way back upstream.

There were cyclists and walkers on the tracks across the

river. They didn't see us. They didn't turn to us.

'Nice day for a paddle!' shouted January.

'Hopeless,' he said, when they just continued on their way.

'Maybe they can't see us,' I said.

'Can't?'

I thought of what Wilson Cairns had said: You have to keep watching, closely, closely, or you'll miss it.

'Maybe they're just not watching closely enough.'

'Ha!' He waved his arms. 'Hey, you lot! Nice day for a paddle!'

But they just ran and cycled on.

We left behind Middens Quay. We passed the other derelict quays on the city's outskirts, the demolition sites and building sites. We passed the great billboards showing how the world would be. The raft tilted and swayed. It was caught by eddies and swerving currents. The dark water slopped across the doors and soaked us. Heaven Eyes held me with her webbed fingers. She gasped as we passed the pubs and clubs and restaurants in Norton. People did watch us now. It was like we'd come back into view. Couples, hand in hand. Family groups. Bunches of lads and bunches of girls. Heaven kept ducking her head down, hiding behind me.

'All them ghosts,' she said. 'All them ghosts!'

The river moved slowly as we reached the limit of the tide. We passed beneath the beautiful steel high-arched bridge. It led to great office blocks, the city's castle, the cathedral with its steeple, the tangle of buildings, new and ancient, stone and timber, concrete and glass squeezed in close together. The city roared and grumbled all around us like a living thing.

Heaven kept pressing her hands to her ears and eyes. She kept taking them away again, to look and listen.

'Feared?' I whispered.

'Feared,' she said.

But her eyes grew wide and fascinated. She began to lift her head, to stretch back, to gaze in wonder at the bridge, at the sky, at the world. And all the time, she gasped and murmured:

'Lovely. Lovely, Erin. Lovely. Lovely. Lovely.'

PART THREE

WHITEGATES

One

Back to where we started from. We paddled through eddies and whirling currents. We steered through floating debris. The sun poured down on us. The river carried us above its deep dark bed and below the endless sky. It carried our stories home with us. It carried our sister home with us. Heaven Eyes. Heaven Eyes. This girl who should have drowned at sea, this girl rescued from the mud, this fishy froggy girl who stared and smiled and saw Heaven at the heart of everything. She gripped my hand. 'Erin,' she said. 'Erin. You will look after me, my best friend?' I smiled and smiled. The raft rocked and spun as we approached the quay. Dark water slopped over us. I kept my eyes on her as we paddled closer. I kept my eyes on her as we reached out and grabbed the timbers and dragged ourselves back to land again. She didn't move, she didn't fade, she didn't disappear. She still held me tight with those webbed fingers. She still smiled into me with those watery eyes. January fastened us with the tethering rope. Mouse climbed up first. Then me. I balanced halfway. Jan passed the sacks and the boxes of Heaven's treasure. I passed them up to Mouse until the raft was empty. January had one foot on the raft, one foot on the timbers. He hauled on the rope. He waited for Heaven Eyes to step across.

She looked up at me. No one spoke. We waited and watched. The raft rocked and gently creaked. My head reeled. I saw Heaven Eyes taken back by the water. I saw the wave that rose and washed her from the raft and washed her back to sea. It was a dream, a vision. When I came out of it, Heaven Eyes crouched there on the doors, on the gilt lettering, on January's curse. She chewed her lips. She trembled. She closed her eyes. Water splashed across her knees.

'Come on,' I said.

'Come on,' said Mouse.

'Be brave, Heaven Eyes,' I said.

'Brave as brave,' said Jan.

The smile crept across her face, across her lips and cheeks. She opened her eyes again, reached up and took my hand. She stepped from the raft and climbed with me.

'Phew!' she said. 'Phew!'

We rested on the ancient quay. January laughed. He leaned over the edge, untied the rope, stood with its end in his fist, restraining the rocking raft.

'What a joke,' he said. 'It was supposed to take us miles away. And we were hardly even out of sight.'

It was true. All the time, we'd been so close to where we'd started from. We could see the jibs of the cranes above the broken rooftops of Black Middens quay. Maybe men in hard hats already walked across the printing floor. Maybe at this very moment they were opening the office door to find Grampa there. Maybe they were already wondering, whispering, starting to tell the tales.

The raft tugged at January, yearning to be set free.

'Let it go,' I said.

'Just let it go?' said January.

His eyes grew wide at the thought of it.

'Just like that?' he said.

'Aye. Just like that.'

He tugged at the rope and grinned.

'Then somebody else'll find it, eh? And set off on their own adventure.'

'Yes,' I said. 'So let it go.'

He handed me the rope.

'Hold on,' he said.

He climbed back down, crouched on the raft, took out his knife, started scratching words in the varnish.

'What you doing?' I shouted.

'If anybody does use it, they need to be prepared,' he said. 'These are their instructions.' He called out the words as he wrote. 'You must take knives, torch, food, a change of clothes. You must be brave and strong. You . . .'

He turned and looked up at me.

'You can't go alone!' I shouted, and he quickly scratched the words.

He turned again.

'You have to take a true friend!' I shouted, and he scratched the words.

'What else?' he said.

I looked down at him. The raft tugged at my hand and yearned to be free.

'Somebody you'd trust your life with,' I said. 'Somebody you'd go as far as death with.'

He smiled and carved these last words deep into the grain.

Then he climbed again and took the rope from my hand.

'OK,' he said, and he let the raft go.

It spun out into the centre of the river and hesitated there, rocking gently, before the flow of the river carried it away. We watched as it became smaller, smaller, smaller. We caught glimpses of the red curse, of the sliding doors, but soon it left our sight. We continued to watch, and in our minds forever after we would see our lovely raft carried past the Ouseburn, over the Black Middens, through the great curve in the river and out into the distant shining sea.

Two

We moved quickly through the ruins, over fences, between great heaps of rubble, past the smouldering remains of bonfires. I was already thinking of the next escape. We'd run away, the four of us together. We'd head for hidden, secret, forbidden places. No need to go far. The most marvellous of things could be found a few yards away, a river's-width away. The most extraordinary things existed in our ordinary world and just waited for us to find them. I held tight on to Heaven Eyes. Seagulls swooped over us with outstretched wings. They soared into our hearts and screamed of freedom. We moved uphill, away from the river, through the wasteland where all the terraces had been knocked down. This was where Mouse had practised his digging, where he had prepared for his great discovery in the black Black Middens. We entered St Gabriel's Estate. We moved past the house where Mum and I had lived. This was where I had grown inside her, where I had been born into our Paradise, where there had been an Oxfam cot and fairies on the wall, bright flowers and fattening gooseberries in the garden, where there had been love and happiness that continued still and would continue ever more. Deep inside me, Mum sighed, whispered my name, shivered with delight. We hurried on, deep into the estate. Brick and pebbledashed walls, red roofs, lamp posts, street names, road signs, square gardens. Sunlight sparkled on the house windows. It bleached the pavements. It shimmered on the black roadway and turned it to a black and shining liquid thing leading us to Whitegates.

'That's where we're heading,' I told Heaven Eyes. 'That building there with three floors and the metal fence around it and the faces at the window.'

Wilson Cairns was at the window, as if he'd been watching ever since we left. Skinny Stu was in the garden with a fag in his mouth and his ribs exposed to the sun, just as when we left.

'Oh, aye?' he said, as we stepped through the iron gate.

'Aye,' we answered.

'Nice picnic, then?'

'Lovely, Stu,' we said.

'And who might this be that you're bringing in?'

'Heaven Eyes,' I said. 'A sister.'

'Oh aye?'

He spat and coughed and crushed his fag beneath his shoe and peered into the sky.

We stepped into Whitegates. Maureen was on the stairs. She gasped when she saw us. She clapped her hand across her mouth.

'Erin!' she said. 'January, Sean! We've been so worried.'

Fingers Wyatt and Maxie Ross watched from the door of the pool room. Fingers grinned at us, held up her hands in joy.

Maureen came down towards us. She reached out and I stepped back. She hugged Mouse. She watched me over his shoulder.

'So worried,' she said. 'Did you not think about that?'

'Yes.'

'But not deeply enough.'

'Anything could have happened to you. Anything. What are we going to do with you?'

'Don't know.'

She moved away from Mouse. She stared at us.

'And who is this?'

'We brought her back with us. She's got no family, no home.'

She regarded Heaven Eyes.

'And what is your name?'

'Go on,' I whispered.

Heaven turned her face towards my arm. She peeped out at Maureen.

'My name is Heaven Eyes. Or Anna.'

'And where are your mother and your father, Anna?'

Heaven drew in her breath in fright. She licked her lips.

'Go on,' I said.

'They is in my sleep thoughts and in my treasures. They is in my thoughts as bright as day.'

Maureen glanced at me.

'And where have you been living, Anna?'

'With my Grampa cross the runny water.'

'And where is your grandfather now?'

Heaven Eyes blinked back tears, couldn't answer.

Maureen moved closer to me.

'Who is she?'

'We don't know.'

She took my hand.

'I dreamed of such awful things, Erin. Why do you feel you need to run from us?'

I looked into her eyes. I saw that she was yearning for an answer. She was yearning to hold me, to welcome me back as a daughter.

'I want to understand,' she said.

'We run for freedom,' I said. 'Just for freedom.'

I turned away and left her standing there.

Three

Fingers hugged me as we went into the pool room. She jabbered our names. She said she'd been so scared that we were at the bottom of the river or the bottom of the sea.

'So many stories,' she said. 'So many rumours. Is it true you went off on a raft?'

'Yes!' we said together.

Fingers chewed her lips. Maxie watched in deep excitement. Others gathered around us and giggled. Fat Kev watched from a corner and scratched his belly.

'I knew,' said Fingers. 'I've been dreaming you. Every night I've seen you rushing down the river. I've seen you miles and miles out at sea.'

She kept laughing, hugging us.

'What was it like?' she kept saying. 'What was it like?'

She kept pausing, staring at Heaven Eyes, wondering.

'Fantastic,' I said. 'The most exciting thing you'd ever know.'

'I knew,' she said. 'I knew. I told you, Maxie, didn't I?'

'She did,' said Maxie. 'A raft. The river. The sea.'

'And how far did you go?' said Fingers.

We hesitated. It seemed nothing to simply say it: across the river, on to the Black Middens, up to Black Middens quay, into the printing works, then home again.

I caught her arm. I gripped her tight.

'Into another world!' I whispered.

She caught her breath.

'No!'

'Yes. We only went across the river but it really was like being in another world.'

Fat Kev clicked his tongue. He sniggered.

I put my arm around Heaven Eyes. I held her at my side.

'And this is our friend who's come back with us. Her name is Heaven Eyes or Anna. She has come to live with us. Heaven, this is Fingers. This is Maxie. These are all your friends.'

She raised her eyes shyly. She smiled shyly. She raised her hand shyly and the light from the windows poured through the webs and made them beautiful. Fingers stretched out and caught her hand.

'You're beautiful,' she said.

'You also is beautiful,' said Heaven Eyes.

She touched the old scalds and burn marks on Fingers' throat.

'You is been hurt,' she said. 'But you is beautiful.'

She gazed more confidently around the room.

'Oh, Erin, my sister,' she said. 'Oh, Erin Law, my sister.'

And then she saw Wilson Cairns. He was at his table,

facing the wall. He had a bowl of clay and a bowl of water. I led her to him. He had the muddy model of a child in his hands. It stood on the table in front of him.

'This is Wilson Cairns,' I said.

I touched his head.

'Hello, Wilson,' I said. 'We came back again, like I said we would.'

He turned. He looked through his thick glasses into Heaven's eyes, deep deep into them, as if he saw right into her, to something astonishing a million miles inside her.

'We kept watching,' I said. 'We saw the most amazing things, Wilson. We found our sister Heaven Eyes and brought her home with us.'

'And you'll leave again,' he said.

'Yes. We'll leave and then come back again. You could leave, as well. You could come with us.'

He sniffed. He looked down at his huge body. A smile crossed his face.

'Me?' he said.

I grinned. I knew he was right. While the rest of us scampered across the earth or drifted away on rafts, he found his own freedom in his way of looking, in his thoughts and dreams, in his way of working clay.

Heaven Eyes reached down and touched the child of clay.

'Is this who you did find in all this water and in all this mud?' she said.

'Yes,' said Wilson.

'Is lovely,' she said.

'Yes.'

'And you has found her sisters and her brothers in all this water and in all this mud?'

'Yes,' said Wilson.

He showed her the other people he had made today: babies and children, boys and girls, some of them already drying out, some of them still soft and wet.

She ran her hands across the wet surfaces. She pressed gently with her fingertips. Clay and water ran and trickled through her hands.

'These is like me,' she said. 'My Grampa did find Heaven Eyes in the black black water and the black black mud.'

Wilson ran his podgy fingers across her silky webs.

'There is things that is lifted out of the water and the mud that do move and walk like us,' she said.

'I know that,' said Wilson.

'We has seen these things. My sister Erin Law and my brothers Janry Carr and Mouse Gullane has seen these things.'

'I know that,' said Wilson.

She stood there with Wilson. She took a ball of clay into her hands. She squeezed and shaped and smiled as the mud and water trickled down her arms. Wilson worked along with her. More bodies emerged out of the clay. Heaven Eyes began to hum a low tune. We backed away from them. We gathered around the pool table and told Fingers, Maxie and the others of our adventures. Fat Kev lumbered out. We saw Maureen watching through the window of her office. We went on talking. We told all the believable parts first. We'd leave the unbelievable till later: Grampa's death, the saint, the full mystery of Heaven Eyes. We went to the window and pointed across the houses of St Gabriel's, past the bridges towards hidden Black Middens quay.

'It was down there, just before a massive curve in the river.'

'Where?' said Maxie.

'Where?' said the others.

'Just past the Ouseburn,' said Mouse.

'Where the mud bank is,' said January. 'The Black Middens. There's old warehouses and factories and a huge printing works. A dead old place. Nobody ever goes there.'

'Till now,' I said.

'Yes, till now,' said January. 'And now they're knocking it down and building restaurants and things, like in all the other places.'

They raised their eyebrows. They shrugged.

'No,' I said. 'We didn't know it was there, either. But it was. An amazing place.' I laughed. 'And now they're knocking it down.'

We stared out together into the estate, into the sunlit afternoon, and the room filled with the amazement that we'd done these things and come back again into our ordinary world, and that the girl discovered in the Black Middens hummed and murmured at our side.

'There's more,' said Fingers. 'Isn't there?'

'Yes,' I said. 'Much more. We'll tell you later.'

Four

'Anna what?' said Maureen.

'We don't know.'

'And she was living with her grandfather?'

'Yes.'

'And he was called?'

'We don't know.'

'And he died?'

'He died.'

'And this was in an old building by the river?'

'A printing works.'

'You know nothing else?'

I shrugged and stood there facing her. She'd called me out of the pool room into the office.

'Please help me,' she said.

'I am helping.'

'Then tell me more. What else do you know?'

'A few things. But they're hers. She might not want you to know them.'

'Oh, Erin.'

'Oh, Erin what?'

'I'm here to help her, like I'm here to help all of you.'

'Help!'

'You've never wanted help, have you? You've always thought you were too strong for it. But we all need help, Erin. All of us.'

I glared.

'You more than anybody else, eh?' I said.

She flinched, but kept her eyes on me.

'Perhaps,' she said.

I wanted to just turn and get out of the place and get back to Jan and Heaven Eyes and all the others. But I stayed there.

'You,' I said.

'Me what?'

'You. You're the one that thinks my mother was no good. You're the one that thinks you could have done better.' I paused while we stared uselessly at each other. 'You're the one that thinks I could have been a daughter for yourself.'

'That was just dreaming,' she whispered. 'Don't you ever see somebody and think, that could have been my father, my sister, my brother . . .'

I clicked my tongue.

'No!' I spat.

'Maybe you will, as you grow older.'

'No, I won't!'

I was trembling. I clenched my fists. I wanted to get out but I couldn't move.

'Yes,' I said. 'Yes I do. Of course I bloody do.'

She reached across the desk to me but I stepped back.

She watched me as I cried, as I sat down on the chair facing her.

'You're such a brave strong girl,' she said softly. 'I know your mother must have been wonderful.'

'She was.'

She reached out again and I flinched again.

'Once upon a time,' she said, 'I dreamed of having lots of children. It wasn't to be. Maybe that's why I came to work in places like this.'

'But you're so cold,' I said. 'It's like you hate us sometimes.'

'There are many disappointments, Erin. Some of you are so so damaged.' She sighed, and her eyes darkened. 'And there are those who simply turn away from your help. Those who simply run away.'

I felt my anger wanting to rise again.

'Like me, you mean.'

'Oh, Erin. Let's not fight.'

I rubbed my eyes. I heard the others laughing in the pool room. My head reeled with the rocking of the raft, the surging of the river.

'We could work together,' said Maureen.

'Eh?'

'We could find out about Heaven Eyes together. We could work out how to care for her. I've seen how you love her, Erin . . . as if she were your sister.'

I knew how useless it could be. Circle times, questions,

counselling, investigations. It would be better to run off with her to the moors, to live up there and run wild and free like vagabonds. Better to make another raft and sail away again towards the sea. There must be other ways to care for children like Heaven Eyes, like myself, like January Carr, like Mouse Gullane.

'Awful things have happened to her,' I said. 'But do you see how happy she is?'

'Yes.'

'But you don't understand that.'

She met my eyes.

'No, I don't. But I could come to understand.'

She reached across the desk. I let her hand fall on mine.

'We could work together,' she said.

I made no answer.

'I'll have to make reports. There'll have to be investigations.'

'Of course there will,' I said. 'You wouldn't know how to just love her, leave her alone and let her be Heaven Eyes, and let her story come out slow as slow.'

'I could try,' she said, and she gripped my hand tightly, but I tugged away and left her.

Five

I carried Heaven Eyes' boxes upstairs with January. We stashed them in my room, on top of my wardrobe. The day was already fading, evening was coming on. We stood at the open window. January was silent, deep in thoughts or dreams. I rested my hand on his shoulder and grinned.

'Don't think we'll be staying long,' I said. 'Got to keep Heaven Eyes out of their clutches, eh?'

He didn't move, didn't speak.

'What is it?' I said.

He blinked, shook his head. It was like he spoke from a thousand miles away.

'Dunno. Nothing.'

I squeezed his arm.

'January?'

'D'you ever feel you're just dead dead young?' he said. 'Like no matter how old you get you're still a little kid, still a baby?'

'Yes.'

'And you get scared,' he said. 'Dead scared?'

'Yes. Dead scared. You're so small, the world's so big. You're like the smallest baby. You're all alone. You wonder what will become of you. You wonder who'll care for you.'

'Yes. Yes.'

I stood there with him. I held his hand and leaned on him. January Carr, my friend. January Carr, this tall strong boy who built the raft that carried us away. January Carr, this tiny baby in a cardboard box on a stormy winter's night. I felt him trembling.

'What is it?' I asked.

'Like something's happening,' he said. 'Like there's something coming that'll . . .'

'That'll what?'

'Dunno,' he said. He chewed his lips. 'I'm scared, Erin. Dead scared.'

'I'll be with you,' I said.

'I know that. I know you love me.'

'And that you love me.'

We stood there, holding each other. And as we stood there, I saw the bird come to the window at his back. It perched on the sill for a second, then flew into the room with a quick fluttering of its wings.

'A *bird*,' he said. 'Look, a bird!'

It circled the room above our heads, a small dark bird, maybe the same curious sparrow I'd seen with Mum. January swivelled his head, followed it with his eyes, goggled in astonishment.

'A *bird*, Erin!'

It went back to the sill, hesitated a moment, then flung itself into the coming night. We watched as it disappeared into the empty air over the estate.

'The bird of life,' I told him.

'Bird of life?'

'It's been before. It comes into the room and out of the room. It spreads its wings and flies about us for a few seconds.'

'And it'll come again?'

'Yes. Mebbe it'll come again.'

We held each other and grinned, and our hearts trembled in wonder at everything we'd seen together.

'Let's go back down,' I said.

'Yes,' he said, but he hesitated. He caught his breath. He closed his eyes. I felt how his spirit rushed into a deep silence again. He shook his head, opened his eyes, looked at me as if he looked from a thousand miles away.

'Hell's teeth, Erin,' he whispered.

'What *is* it, Jan?'

'Dunno, Erin. Dunno.'

We crossed the landing, went downstairs, went into the pool room. Wilson and Heaven Eyes still faced the wall, working the clay. They leaned together, the slender girl and the huge boy. Muddy water trickled from their fingers. The falling sunlight slanted in from outside. The children playing pool were dark bowed figures with fragments of dust shimmering around them. As I approached, I heard how Heaven and Wilson breathed together, how their breath was like a song, a low sweet chant. Their heads were tilted forward. They were engrossed in the clay, in their fingers that smoothed and stretched and shaped the clay. January was behind me, standing with Maxie at the pool table. A bird sang in the concrete garden. The distant city roared. I felt the river running through my mind. I felt the swirl and rush of deep dark water and the long slow drag of tides. Heaven giggled as I moved closer. Wilson sighed with joy. I looked down and saw the little figure stretched between their hands. It was the wet sloppy figure of a child. Legs and arms, a glistening body. It trembled. There were tiny spasms in its arms, its legs. Wilson eased it away from his palms and held it with his fingertips. The body arched, the head tilted back, the arms gently rose, a leg stretched forward, just as if it was about to dance. Heaven laughed. Wilson sighed. It was joined to their fingers just by a gooey paste, paste like at the edge of the Black Middens, where mud and water mingled, where the most mysterious of creatures – Heaven Eyes, the saint – could be discovered. The figure came to rest, and Wilson laid it on the wet surface of the unused clay.

I reached past him and touched the cold wet clay child. I touched the child that had been conjured out of clay and water and love and hope.

'You see?' he said.

'Yes. Yes. Yes.'

Six

'I want her to stay in my room tonight,' I said.

She just shrugged.

'I'll put blankets and things on the floor.'

She just shrugged.

'Anything,' she said.

She turned her eyes away.

'Maybe I've always been wrong,' she said.

'What?'

'Maybe I could never get to know you all, never get to understand you all.'

I looked down and shrugged.

'Maybe it's time for *me* to leave,' she said.

'Maybe.'

She caught her breath and I heard how such a simple word caused such pain.

'But I have tried to love you all,' she said. 'Not always in the right way, perhaps . . .'

I could see she needed reassurance, but I just shrugged again.

'It's OK, then?' I said. 'About Heaven Eyes.'

'Anything.'

We got some blankets and pillows and laid them on the floor beside my bed. We sat together against the wall below the window and the night air flowed over us and the moon shone down on us. We held hands and drifted through our memories and dreams. She gazed into the faces of her lost family. I opened my treasure box and put on the lipstick, the nail varnish, the perfume. I gazed at the photograph of the fishy froggy thing inside my Mum. 'Mum,' we whispered together. 'Mum. Mum.' We smiled as our mothers came whispering our names, as they gently touched our skin, as they cradled us in their arms. We drifted away from the little room in Whitegates. I was in the garden filled with flowers and fattening gooseberries. Where was Heaven Eyes? On a sofa on her mother's knee, perhaps, or on a little sailing boat that danced beneath the sun. We drifted, drifted, drifted. January brought us out of it. He gently opened the door and came in to us. He crouched in front of us, his face lit and shadowed by the moon.

'Couldn't settle,' he said. 'Couldn't sleep.'

'Janry Carr,' said Heaven Eyes.

'Yes?'

She squeezed my hand.

'Tell me bout myself.'

We opened a box and Jan took out a newspaper.

'What is these things saying?' she said.

I sighed. One day we would have to tell her everything we

knew. We would lead her towards it slowly, slowly.

'Your name is Anna May,' said Jan.

'Anna May?

'Yes. Anna May.'

'Anna May. Is a nice name, Anna May?'

'Yes,' I told her. 'Is a nice name.'

'I know other things,' said January. 'But we'll tell you slowly.'

'Yes,' said Heaven Eyes. 'Slow as slow.'

She rolled the name around her lips and tongue and throat.

'Anna May, Anna May, Anna May . . .

'May is a time of year,' I said. 'A time when the world gets stronger and brighter.'

'Anna May,' she said. 'Anna May. Anna May.' She laughed. 'Does feel that funny in my mouth.'

Outside, across the river, the city gently roared. We heard footsteps above us, footsteps on the stairs, footsteps outside my door. A tapping at the door, and Mouse slipped shyly in.

'Couldn't sleep,' he said.

We laughed and he sat beside us. Squeak scuttled across his opened hands.

'Eek. Eek.'

'You going away again?' said Mouse.

'Some time,' I said.

'You'll let me know.'

'Don't worry, Mouse. We'll let you know. You'll come with us.'

We sat there. Our heads were filled with the river, the

black Black Middens, the printing works, the saint and Grampa stepping down into the tide.

'Mouth more, Janry Carr,' said Heaven Eyes.

'More?'

'More secret things, my brother Janry Carr.'

'Your mother was called Alison. Your father was called Thomas.'

'Names,' she said. 'Lovely names.'

I squeezed her hand.

'Lovely names,' I told her.

'They is still as still?' she said.

January sighed.

'Yes, Heaven. We think they are still as still.'

Tears trickled on her cheeks.

'Still as still,' she said. 'But they do move and smile and shiver in my thoughts and they is bright as day.'

She held her hands up and the moonlight streamed through them and they were beautiful.

'Fishy froggy,' she whispered. 'Fishy froggy Anna. Mouth more, mine brother Janry Carr.'

'Your sister was called Caroline. Your brothers were Anthony and Tom.'

More tears trickled on her cheeks, splashed into her lap. I held her close.

'They is still as still,' she said. 'And little Heaven Eyes is all alone and this world is big as big as big as big.'

I held her tight as the secrets entered her, as the story deepened in her.

'I am your sister,' I said. 'These are your brothers. We love you. We love you.'

She leaned against me.

'Mouth no more, my brother,' she said. 'Mouth no more till this night is bright as day.'

Seven

We slept, the four of us sitting there in the moonlight beneath the window. It seemed like a dream when Maureen tapped at the door and stepped shyly into the room. She stood in a long blue dressing gown. Her feet were bare. Her face was pale as the moon.

'I'm sorry,' she said. 'Couldn't sleep . . .'

I stared at her. January stared at her. She hesitated in the doorway.

'I worried about you all,' she said. 'I . . . I thought you'd all gone off again . . .'

Her voice faltered. She flicked at her eyes with her fingers. She crouched in front of us. She reached out and took Heaven's hand. Leave her alone! I wanted to say. But I saw Heaven's hand close gently around Maureen's.

'We will find you,' Maureen whispered. 'We'll search the records of missing children and we'll find someone like you.

She delicately touched the webs on Heaven's fingers. Her breath quivered.

'Who do you think you are?' she said.

'My name is Anna May.'

'Anna May?'

'Anna May. There is other things, but they come slow as slow as slow.'

'We know other things,' said January. 'But they're things for Heaven Eyes to know. Mebbe she'll tell you one day. OK?'

He tilted his head to one side.

'OK?' he said.

'OK,' she said.

Go on, I wanted to say. Go on. Get out!

As if she had heard me, she said softly, 'Erin. Please don't.'

She stayed there, crouching before Heaven Eyes, like she was wanting something, waiting for something.

Heaven Eyes touched Maureen's face.

'Where is your little girl?' she asked.

Maureen stared.

'My little girl?'

'Yes. The mum of Erin had a little girl. The mum of Heaven Eyes had a little girl. Where is the little girl that was in Maureen?'

The tears shone in Maureen's eyes and reflected the moon.

'There is no little girl,' she said.

Heaven pondered this.

'Then Maureen is the little girl. So where is the mum of Maureen?'

The tears dripped and shone.

'There is no mum,' said Maureen.

'Still as still?' said Heaven Eyes.

'Still as still. Still as still.'

The webbed fingers stroked Maureen's cheeks, they wiped away the tears. I looked across at Jan. We rolled our eyes in scorn, then in wonder.

'You is lovely,' said Heaven Eyes. 'You is lovely, Maureen.'

Eight

We drifted in and out of sleep and dreams. I felt the lovely rocking of the river, the lovely spinning of the raft. In deepest sleep I went down into the blackness of the Middens and lay there with my Mum and many saints. I swam with shoals of fish, with frogs. I kicked my arms and legs and heard Mum singing to me and felt her hands pressing in on me. I flew in and out of rooms with little curious birds and flew into the night again and headed for my nest. I spread my hands like Heaven Eyes and held their webs up to the sun and moon. I felt the hands of Wilson Cairns supporting me, felt his breath on me, felt him urging me to move, to walk across a little table while fascinated children gathered all around. I felt the heart beating in me, the spirit shivering with life and love in me. I heard my whispered name, 'Erin. Erin. Erin.' Opened my eyes.

'Erin,' Jan whispered. 'What is it?'

'Nothing. Just need to move. Need you to come with me.'

'What is it, Jan?'

'Please, Erin.'

We left the room, tiptoed down through the house. It was soon after dawn. The sun was burning low in the east. We went out across the concrete, through the iron gate, into the estate. Sparrows dashed across the sky. There were pigeons and crows, seagulls wheeling and screaming high above. We passed the little house, the beaten garden, the scratched door. Came to the waste land. Sunlight gleamed on the arch of the greatest bridge. The city's low rumble as its day began. Its roofs, its spires, its curving steep streets and tumbling steps and alleyways, its brick and steel and stone. Its jagged silhouette. The distant moors bulging in the east. Sky brightening, brightening, brightening. The scents of petrol, seaweed, sea, fish, rot, flowers, dust. Mysterious river glowing like beaten metal above its deep dark bed and below the endless sky. River heaving through the city, over the black Black Middens, rushing down towards the sea. River rushing past new pubs and clubs and offices, past ancient warehouses, ruined quays, huge cranes, construction sites. Mysterious river rushing through the present and the past and surging to the future. We sat on a pile of bricks and rubble and gazed out at it all.

'What is it, Jan?' I said.

'Dreams. Just dreams. Cardboard boxes and hospitals and stormy nights. But stronger than before.'

He shuddered.

'Scary,' he said.

'Scary.'

For a moment I trembled with my own scary dreams.

'Jan,' I said. 'Is it awful being us?'

'Dunno,' he said. 'What's it like being anybody? But aye, sometimes it's awful. Sometimes it's the worst thing in the world.'

'Let's run away,' I said. 'Let's go tomorrow. Today.'

'Aye.'

'Where to?'

'The moors?'

'Aye, the moors. Just imagine it, eh?'

We stared at the moors and dreamed ourselves there, striding through bracken, skipping over little streams, lying beneath the sun on soft green turf, surrounded by the calls of curlews and the scent of peat.

'Wow!' I said.

'Wow! Wow!'

We giggled.

'Jan,' I said. 'Think we'll always run away?'

'Dunno. Till we're older, mebbe. Mebbe till there's kids of our own we want to care for.'

For an instant I saw it, me and Jan together years in the future with little kids beside us. Just for an instant, just a glimpse. I didn't speak it, but I thought that maybe Jan had glimpsed it, too.

'Might be awful,' I said. 'But I love it just the same.'

'Love what?'

'Being alive, being me, in this world, here and now.'

He grinned.

'It's bloody great, eh?' he said. 'Bloody great.'

We stood up and wandered across the waste land towards the estate. The sun continued rising. Jan held my arm, stopped me. He turned and peered back to where we'd come from.

'What's up?' I said.

'Dunno. Nothing.'

We walked on and he kept turning, turning.

'We're not asleep?' he said.

'We're not asleep.'

'So why do the dreams keep on coming, Erin?'

Nine

Whitegates. The iron gate, the concrete garden. Wilson stared from the window, like he stared past us, through us, to something a million miles away. January kept on turning as we walked towards it, as we entered the gate, as we drifted to the door. He looked back as if there was something following us, tracking us, seeking us. We went inside. Deep silence. We sat in the pool room behind Wilson. Dust seethed and glittered in the sunlight that poured through the windows. January became dead calm. He held my hand.

I peered into his eyes.

'What is it?'

'Just stay with me,' he said. 'Stay beside me, Erin.'

Then footsteps upstairs, above our heads. I turned and saw Heaven Eyes and Mouse coming down together. Heaven raised her hand and beamed at me. Mouse yawned, rubbed his eyes. Maureen came behind them in her dressing gown and bare feet, her hair hanging loose and tangled. She stood in the doorway as Mouse and Heaven came to us. We watched each other. Our eyes were wary, suspicious, but I knew that we had begun to move closer to each other. I knew that our story had begun to change. I sighed and thought of Mum and I felt her smiling.

'Janry Carr,' said Heaven Eyes. 'My brother. You is far as far away?'

He gazed at her from his dream.

'Janry Carr is good as good,' she said. 'Strong as strong.'

She sat on the floor with Mouse. They played with Squeak. Deep inside, Mum sang to me.

A deep sigh from Wilson Cairns. Then another. January went to the window and stood beside him. I went to his shoulder. He reached back and took my hand and drew me to his side.

'Erin,' he breathed.

We watched the estate: the pale houses, the shimmering roadways, the green gardens, the red rooftops, the birds flickering and wheeling across the great sky. We watched in silence and we waited.

She must have come across the waste land above the river, past the little house and garden. She came into sight, stood at the junction of two streets. She wore blue jeans, a black leather jacket and carried a red rucksack on her back, as if she'd come back from some adventure. She looked about her until she saw Whitegates. She watched it for a time. Her fair hair lifted in the breeze and blew about her face. She looked back to where she'd come from and seemed about to go back again, but she came onwards. She was still hesitant, still kept looking back, but then she straightened her shoulders and shook her head so that her hair swung and we saw her earrings glittering. She walked more quickly, more purposefully. The black road at her feet shone like liquid and her feet seemed to step in and out of liquid, over liquid. Closer to, as she approached the iron gate, we saw her red lipstick, pale lined face, troubled bright eyes. Her clothes were dusty. A ripped knee in her jeans. A tear in her jacket. We saw how scared she was, how worn she was, but we saw how right January was. She was beautiful. She stepped into the concrete garden. She saw us at the window, and hesitated again in fear and trepidation.

'Oh, Erin!' whispered Jan.

'Keep watching,' murmured Wilson Cairns.

No trembling in January's hands, no quiver in his breath, just a deep deep silence in him as she came on again and entered Whitegates. I walked with him from the window. Heaven watched with her lovely eyes that saw through all the trouble in the world to the heaven that lies beneath. She touched January with her webbed fingers as he passed.

She stood there, in the hallway.

How did they know each other? Ancient dreams. Images from a stormy winter's night. Love. They watched each other.

'I knew you'd come,' said Jan.

She raised her hands to her cheeks and stared across them.

'I waited for you,' he whispered.

I tried to leave him there but he held me tight.

'It's all right,' he said. 'I know you've always loved me. I always knew you'd come back for me.'

'What's your name?'

He caught his breath.

'I don't know.' He let me go. 'Tell me what my name is.'

They moved across the little hall towards each other and I turned away.

I sat with Heaven Eyes and held her hand. Mouse sat at our side and played with Squeak. Wilson worked his clay. Soon, Fingers and Maxie and the others would come down to us. Outside, the day intensified.

'Was the mum of Janry Carr,' said Heaven Eyes.

'Yes. That's right. The mum of January Carr.'

'Is a lovely mum.'

'Yes.'

We sighed and smiled. She wriggled against me.

'Tell the tale of Janry Carr,' she whispered.

'Oh, it's a wintry stormy tale,' I said.

'You'll tell it?'

'Yes, Heaven Eyes. One day I'll tell you the tale.'

Ten

Once upon a time, when my story started, I was a tiny thing, an invisible thing, the tiniest thing in the whole wide world. I was hidden deep down in the dark inside my Mum. We were in a cheap bed-and-breakfast place above the quay. My Mum was beautiful, with brilliant green eyes and red hair that grew like fire around her lovely face. My Dad was a sailor from a foreign trawler that had come up river to shelter from a storm at sea. As she watched him sail away from us, my Mum already felt me trembling with life inside her. She took me to a little house in St Gabriel's Estate. I turned into the fishy froggy thing that kicked and swam inside her. She sang to me and whispered to me. She bought an Oxfam cot and put pictures on the walls and prepared a Paradise for me. We lived in that Paradise for a few short years, and then she died. It could have been a sad sad tale. All stories could be sad sad tales: the stories of my friends, January Carr, Mouse Gullane, Anna May, Wilson Cairns and of all the others. But they are not sad tales. We have each other, and our stories mix and mingle like the twisting currents of a river. We hold each other tight as we spin and lurch across our lives. There are moments of great joy and magic. The most astounding things can lie waiting as each day dawns, as each page turns. When I turned away from January that morning and went back into the pool room, I knew that one story was ended. It was the story of what happened when we sailed away from Whitegates, of how we met Heaven Eyes on the black Black Middens and brought her home with us. There are endings of a kind: January Carr now lives with his Mum in St Gabriel's Estate and he is called Gabriel Jones; Maureen tells us we are beautiful and brave and she tries to believe it; Heaven Eyes lives here with us, and we call her Anna May. We slowly slowly tell her the few things that can be known about her life. We hold her hands and tell her about the lovely family lost at sea. We have begun to decipher Grampa's books, to disentangle his strange tale from lists of discoveries in the Black Middens, from the drawings and maps and sketches that pack the margins. The black writing takes us back and back, back to a time when the printing works was filled with work and noise, when great ships steamed on the river and men in overalls packed the quays. Their story flows into the tale of Heaven Eyes, who was lifted by a caretaker from the Black Middens on a moony night, then into the tale of three creatures who might have been angels, might have been devils, but were probably something in between. Like all stories, it has no true end. It goes on and on and mingles with all the other stories in the world. This has just been our part of it. You might not believe it. But everything is true.